# Farewell to Forever

**STEVEN TORRES**

# A Love Letter To My Readers



I hope that you're doing well in whichever location of the world you're currently in. The inspiration for my novel was to craft a love story in which readers could see themselves reflected in the characters. My goal is for you to find something meaningful within their journey. This project is a labor of love, born from my deep desire to achieve a dream I've had since my teenage years: to self-publish a contemporary romance novel.

I hope that whatever you are pursuing in your life right now is driven by love. The world needs more people who are passionate about their endeavors, who show kindness to strangers, and who embrace love and compassion. We need people who celebrate our differences and who love themselves so profoundly that they can share that love with others. The world needs more people like you.

Thank you for choosing love. Be kind to yourself and to others. I believe in you. I'm proud of you. I love you.

With love,

Steven Torres

# Chapter 1
## The Night That Changed It All

Music is a universal language, weaving together rhythm, melody, and emotion into a tapestry of sound that transcends cultural and temporal boundaries. It is the soundtrack of our lives, marking moments in time within the vast universe we inhabit. As the beat pulses around me, I can't help but move, the soundwaves creating a rush of dopamine. In the middle of a vibrant crowd, my best friend and I dance to the electric beats of EDM. This is the start of spring for us—a moment where we can truly be ourselves.

The crowd looked like a sea of people. Everywhere you looked, people were dancing, jumping, raising their hands in the air, or simply having a good time. The outdoor-centered stage embraced the thousands of spectators. Three huge screens displayed colorful visuals while laser lights beamed over the crowd. The Chainsmokers played their music as we freely moved to every rhythm emanating from the large speakers surrounding the stage.

Dylan looked directly into my eyes as we sang every lyric to each song. What a beautiful bond and experience we had. Dylan and I met in our freshman year of college. I was an introvert, and he was the fun, bright breath of fresh air that made me want to be his best friend. We always had a great time together. He balances my personality and brings out the best in me. Tonight, we had one of my favorite nights together  in a long time.

As the performance ended, we moved away from the stage and headed towards a burger and fries kiosk to grab something to eat.

"Girl! I saw you throwing it back a few times. I didn't know you were THAT FLEXIBLE," Dylan said.

"Really?" I replied, trying to hold back my laugh.

"Yes! Who was she?" he asked with a sassy attitude.

"I guess I was having a good time," I said, looking over my shoulder and pouting my lips.

"Uh-huh. We left everything on that grass. You need to bring her out more often. She was everything! The hair flips, the hip movements, and those fist pumps—those were a thing of their own," he said, laughing.

"Those were my power moves. I'm surprised no one asked me for my number after those sexy dance moves," I said sarcastically.

"It was giving main character energy. You ate that!" he said, smiling.

We both laughed.

We were next in line, and we both ordered the same burger with cheese, caramelized onions, and ketchup, along with a medium-sized side of fries. We also got beers in plastic cups. We found an outdoor picnic table and sat down to eat.

"How has your semester been going so far?" I asked while dipping a fry into some ketchup.

"I'm doing pretty well, actually. It has been a lot of work, but I think I've established a study schedule that works for me. My first two years were awful, though. I had no idea what I was doing. But I can't complain. Psychology is something I'm truly passionate about, and I've been loving it so far," he said.

"What about you? Are you still doubting your major?" he asked.

"Sadly, I am. It's hard because, deep down, I know I wanted to pursue something in a creative field. For some reason, I ended up studying accounting—the most boring career ever. I feel like I'm definitely going to regret my choice in the long run. But it's a bit late now that I have only a year left until graduation," I said.

"It's never too late to start over. Maybe you can start working in your field and use it as a stepping stone to accomplish a new goal," he suggested.

"You're right. You always have a positive perspective on everything. I love that about you. You definitely keep me grounded," I said, grateful for his words.

"If not, wait for me until I become a full ass doctor, and we can get married, and I'll take care of you," he said.

"But you are extremely gay," I said.

"It doesn't matter. We can have a slumber party every night. We can paint our nails and shit. Can you imagine all the facials and nighttime routines we could do together? That's life right there! Who wouldn't love that? No sex, though. That would be my last straw," he said, laughing.

I almost choked while drinking my beer.

"I love you. Thank you for being my friend. Thanks for existing," I said seriously.

"You're more than welcome. I love you too. Should we head out?" he asked.

I looked at my phone, and it was 2:53 a.m.

On our drive home, we felt so exhausted that we could fall asleep at any minute. We kept the music on just to make sure we stayed awake. There was not much traffic at three in the morning, and the streets looked like a ghost town. The peaceful atmosphere made it seem as if Earth was taking a break from the constant chaos of humans.

"I had a blast with you today," I said.

"It was so much fun," he agreed, nodding.

"We should do this more often during the summer," I suggested.

"Definitely! Bring back all those moves you have. The world needs to see more of you like that," he said, smiling at me.

"More like what?" I asked, curious about what he was going to say.

"Being a hundred percent yourself. You seem so happy tonight. We need to see her more often. Don't overthink life; just try your best. Do what's best for you, and everything will work out in the best possible way," he genuinely expressed.

For some reason, his words touched my soul deeply, comforting me for a moment.

"I'm glad I get to experience life with you. You are the best! I should marry you tomorrow," I said, smiling.

"Girl! I can't. I'm busy. I have things to do," he said jokingly.

We both smiled, but at this point, laughing felt more like a chore because of how tired we were.

"Can't wait till we get home. I'm going to sleep..." I said, focusing on the road.

All of a sudden, a cast of white light appeared out of nowhere towards us.

"Careful!" I screamed.

I felt the car swerving and going off the road. I tried to hold on to my seat as much as I could, but everything happened so fast. My heart started pounding. I tried to scream. I took a deep breath, thinking it might be my last, all while watching a tree ahead of us come closer with each passing millisecond. The last thing I heard was a loud crunching noise. Small pieces of glass struck my face as I slowly closed my eyes. Everything went into complete darkness. Not a single outside noise. Not a single beat of music.

## Chapter 2
## Silent Tears

I gingerly open my eyes, greeted by a stark unfamiliarity. The room envelops me in a disconcerting silence, broken only by the persistent beep emanating from a monitor beside the bed where I lie. My gaze shifts to my left arm, where an intravenous line snakes into my veins, a tether to the unknown. With deliberate slowness, I turn my head, surveying my surroundings. My right hand comes into view, and I tentatively flex my fingers, an attempt to reconnect with my body.

Yet, a pervasive numbness persists, stealing sensation and leaving behind a disquieting emptiness. Panic begins to bubble within me as I cast a desperate glance towards the side of my bed, where my mother sits, her weariness evident in the lines etched upon her face.

"Mom," I rasp, my voice barely audible in the stillness.

"Swee- sweetie, you're awake," she responds, her exhaustion palpable.

"I can't... I can't feel my legs," I confess, the words tasting of fear as they leave my lips. I attempt to coax movement from my toes, but they remain stubbornly unresponsive, as if shrouded in a deep slumber.

A wave of claustrophobia washes over me, the realization of my lack of control sending me spiraling into despair. Tears blur my vision, their presence a bitter reminder of my vulnerability. I've endured physical pain before, but nothing compares to the ache that now grips my heart.

In an instant, the future I had envisioned crumbles before me, its once-clear path obscured by an impenetrable haze. I am adrift in a sea of uncertainty, the weight of my newfound reality pressing down upon me like a suffocating darkness. Loneliness wraps its icy tendrils around me, suffusing the room with its chilling embrace.

My mother's touch offers little solace as I struggle to make sense of the chaos raging within me. Her words are lost amidst the cacophony of my own anguish, leaving me adrift in a world devoid of comprehension.

Desperation drives her from the room, her frantic cries echoing in the empty space.

"Nurse! Nurse!" She calls her voice a lifeline in the void.

A flurry of activity ensues as a figure clad in white enters the room, their presence a beacon of hope amidst the uncertainty. With practiced ease, they reassure me that everything will be alright, their words a soothing balm to my fractured soul.

As the unknown medicine flows through my veins, a sense of calm descends upon me, offering respite from the storm that rages within.

Emerging from what felt like a mere slumber, the grim reality of my situation crashes over me once more. The specter of never again traversing the world on my own two feet looms ominously in my mind, a silent tormentor.

Tears well in my eyes, yet this time they fall in silence, a testament to the depth of my despair. Beside me, my mother remains a steadfast presence, her comforting touch a lifeline in the darkness.

"We'll find a way through this," she murmurs, her voice a soothing refrain. "Together, just like we always have."

I cling to her words, desperate for reassurance in the face of overwhelming uncertainty.

"What did the doctors say?" I inquire, my voice trembling with apprehension.

"You sustained a spinal cord injury," she replies, her voice heavy with sorrow. "The accident fractured your T12 vertebrae. They say there's a chance, with therapy, you could regain mobility."

The weight of her words settles heavily upon me, the enormity of my situation crashing down with unbearable force. "Why me?" I whisper, the question a desperate plea for understanding.

"It was an accident, Madison," she responds, her own tears mirroring my anguish. In that moment, we are united in our grief, two souls bound together by the cruel hand fate has dealt us.

"Where's Dylan?" My voice is a trembling desperation.

"He sadly didn't make it." Those words hit my soul to the core.

Closing my eyes felt like a desperate cry for help. Every teardrop is a reaction to my emotional pain. I wish I could forget how to breathe.

As I gaze into my mother's tear-streaked face, I find solace in the unspoken promise of her unwavering love. Though the road ahead may be fraught with challenges, we will navigate it together, drawing strength from each other as we journey into the unknown.

# Chapter 3
## A New Beginning

As we returned from the hospital to my new world and new reality, I went directly to my bedroom. I was emotionally and physically drained. I asked my father to help me get into bed so I could rest a little. As I lay in bed, I stared at my surroundings. It felt like forever since my stay in the hospital, and everything reminded me of how life was before my accident.

My room is my cozy space, where every detail reflects who I am as a person. The neutral white walls and my light oak bed frame create a calming atmosphere. My record player sits on top of my dresser, while a disco ball rests in a corner of the room. A framed poster of a beach on one of the walls adds a splash of color to the otherwise light walls. My favorite part of the room is the window that overlooks the lush green grass of our backyard. I've spent hours staring through that window since we moved into this house.

As I finished assessing every corner of my room, I stared at the temporary wheelchair provided by my medical insurance. I immediately started tearing up. For some reason, I hated that thing. I am still in denial that this is now my new reality. When I thought everything was going according to plan, this incident came and knocked down every single domino I had aligned for my future. It filled me with so much anger. What now? How am I going to navigate this? Will I ever go back to how my life was? I just lay there, staring at the ceiling, overwhelmed and occasionally wiping away my tears with my hands.

A few days have passed, and I'm trying to adapt to my new life. Every single task that I used to do by myself now takes double the time and effort. Transferring from my bed to my chair, getting dressed, and sometimes even the smallest challenges I face throughout the day make me want to give up. Some days, I feel like I can take on the world, and other days, I feel like I don't want to exist anymore.

Today was my first day of physical therapy. As I was sitting on the side of my bed, my dad came in and sat next to me.

"Are you excited for your first day of therapy?" he asked, with a huge smile on his face.

"Excited for what?" I responded, my tone dripping with frustration.

"I don't know. Maybe you'll learn a few new dance moves," he said, trying to be funny.

"Dad, it's physical therapy, not a salsa dance class," I said. My voice sounded like a teenager going through puberty, but deep down, I knew he was trying to make me feel better.

Silence filled the room for a few seconds as we both stared out the window.

"Whatever you do today, give it your all like you always do," he said, abandoning his humor. "No matter how difficult it feels, you know that I'm here for you and always will be."

"Thanks, Dad. I'm going to try my best," I said, grateful for his encouraging words.

He gave me a side hug and kissed me on the head.

"I love you," he said, with a sincere look in his eyes.

"I love you too, Dad," I replied, grateful for his support.

He got up from the bed, did the cringiest dance move I had seen in a while, and said, "When you come back from therapy, you better be showing off your cool and hip dance moves."

He did another unknown dance move, which honestly made me laugh—it had been a long time since something made me feel that content.

"Bye, sweetie. Let me know how it goes," he said, raising his hand as he stood in the doorway.

"Oh, I will!" I responded, with a more hopeful tone.

I transferred from my bed to my wheelchair and went to my closet to grab what I was going to wear for my therapy session. I picked out some black leggings, my favorite lavender sweatshirt, and a pair of white sneakers. Putting on clothes has been a new challenge for me. I found that transferring back to my bed and putting my pants on there is much easier than trying to put them on in my wheelchair. Using my upper body strength, I can get my pants over my hips and butt without them getting stuck on my thighs. It takes double the effort it used to, but I'm learning to adapt to my new life.

As I finished getting dressed, I went to my bathroom to fix my hair. These days, pulling my brunette wavy hair into a ponytail is good enough for me. I finished getting ready, took one last look in the mirror, and noticed how unhappy I looked. I took a deep breath and met up with my mom in the kitchen for breakfast.

# Chapter 4
## Bibliotherapy

Stepping outside the house brings a refreshing sense of freedom and joy. This is my first time getting out of the house in my wheelchair. Today, it's a crisp sixty-degree spring day here in North Carolina. It has been raining for the past few days. I have always loved rainy days for some reason—the cool breeze, the earthy smell of nature, and the soothing gray skies create the perfect atmosphere for cuddling up in bed with a good book. As I settled into the car, my mom carefully placed my wheelchair in the back seat.

"Mom, after therapy, can we go to the bookstore? I'd like to find something to keep my mind off things, if you don't mind," I said.

"We can do that. I need to stop by the grocery store in the same outlet mall anyway," Mom agreed.

During our car ride, I couldn't help but stare out the window at the little droplets cascading down the glass.

As we pass through our neighborhood, I see beautiful green trees everywhere—something I completely ignored before my accident. I feel like my life has slowed down for a moment, and now I catch myself constantly noticing the small things in life. Maybe that's how my life is going to feel from now on. A small insignificant life. Perhaps everything that happened to me has a reason for it, but that's something I may never understand.

"Are you excited to start your physical therapy today?" Mom asked.

"Nervous would be a better word for it," I replied.

"Why do you feel nervous about it?" she asked.

"I just don't want to get my hopes up. Every time I meet with a different doctor, they say there's a small possibility that I could walk again. I don't believe that's true," I said.

"Who knows? We just have to wait and see what happens. Whatever the outcome, I'm here for you. Your dad and I are here for you. Just remember that," she said.

"Thanks, Mom," I said.

"Have you thought about going back to college to continue your semester in the fall?" she asked.

"I don't know. That's the farthest thing from my mind right now," I said, staring out the window.

"I mean, your life didn't end because of your accident. As long as we're here, we have to try our best to keep moving forward no matter what. I know it must be hard dealing with all of this, but the last thing we can do is give up on life. You are a strong woman. I've seen how hard you've worked to achieve the things you always wanted. Don't let life rob you of that. Today, during your physical therapy, give it your all. Do it for you!" she said.

Her words made me a little teary-eyed.

"I'm going to try my best," I said.

I took a quick glance at her; she was trying to wipe away her tears while keeping both hands on the steering wheel.

We made it to the rehabilitation center. Waiting for my turn felt like a lifetime. The anticipation was feeding my anxiety levels. All of a sudden, I heard, "Madison Henderson!" from the ceiling speakers. My mom and I met with my physical therapist, who gave us a rundown of what I would be working on during my therapy session. I also got to meet my physical therapy nurse, Shelby. She is the sweetest human being I have ever encountered. She made me feel welcomed and excited to embark on my new therapy journey.

We worked on some stretching exercises, most of which were focused on measuring the strength in my upper body. They had me stretch my arms in different directions and examined my core stability.

After an hour of therapy, we left the center.

"I wasn't that bad. Hopefully, I'll regain more strength during my future visits. I'm actually excited about the process," I said, feeling more optimistic as I pushed myself through the parking lot.

"I'm glad you have a positive outlook on it. I'm really proud of you," Mom said, taking the car keys out of her purse.

"Thank you! Are we going to the grocery store now?" I asked.

"While I do the groceries, I can drop you off at the bookstore if you want," she suggested.

"I'm excited. I haven't stepped foot inside a Barnes & Noble in months," I said.

We arrived at the bookstore. Mom got my wheelchair out of the car, and I transferred myself into it.

"Meet you in forty minutes. Text me when you're done," Mom said through the passenger window.

"I will. Bye!" I said.

I rolled to the front of Barnes & Noble and looked for the accessible push button. As I entered, I couldn't help but notice the fresh scent of new books, the huge rows of bookshelves, and the different genre labels on every shelf. I went straight to the romance aisle. As I skimmed through the sea of pastels and colorful books, I couldn't help but admire the beautiful covers. Every single book, crafted by someone, never fails to bring the novelty of searching for the perfect story in which I want to lose myself. That sense of escapism we all look for.

After rolling through the aisles, I decided to check the nonfiction section to see if I could find a book that could help me navigate my new reality. The shelves were packed with all sorts of self-help books. I grabbed one and read the title: *Become Rich Before Your 30s*. I quickly put it back on the shelf and grabbed another one: *Dirt Poor Mentality*. Jeez, what's up with all these "make a lot of money" books? As I continued looking through the covers, one title grabbed my attention: *Overcoming Adversity: 5 Steps to a Happier Life*. The book was on a higher shelf. I probably should ask for help, but I'm afraid of bothering someone, so I went for it. I faced the bookshelf, put my wheelchair brakes on, and with my left hand tried to push myself up. I struggled a bit, but managed to push the book to the edge when, all of a sudden, a few books came crashing down to the floor.

"Let me help you with that," I heard a guy say.

"I'm so sorry," I said, feeling embarrassed as I picked up the books from the floor.

"Don't worry about it. It happens to the best of us," he said.

As I handed him some of the books, I noticed how handsome he was. He looked around my age, with dark brown almond-shaped eyes and a perfectly clean-shaven jawline. His medium-tone brown hair fringe perfectly framed his face. After he finished putting the books back on the shelf, he asked me, "Is this the one you wanted?"

I nodded.

"Here you go," he said, finishing up by putting the remaining copies where they belonged.

"Not feeling satisfied with life?" he asked.

"What?" I replied, confused by his question.

"Your book choice," he said, smiling.

"Oh. Aren't we all? We all need a little more happiness in our lives these days," I said.

"We sure do. I'm Benson, by the way. And you are?" he asked, offering his hand for me to shake.

"Madison," I replied, shaking his hand.

"Nice to meet you, Madison! Are you from around here?" he asked, making eye contact.

"Yeah. I actually live about twenty minutes from here," I said, trying not to stumble over my words.

"Nice. Do you come here often?" he asked.

"Four to five times a year. I try to limit myself from purchasing new books all the time. It can be really addicting," I said.

He smiled.

"What about you?" I asked.

"I recently got into reading and I'm searching for something that piques my interest," he said, glancing at some books on the shelf.

"You're in a good aisle to start with. There's nothing like relating to real-life stories or taking advice from people who seem to have their lives together," I said, holding my book on my lap.

"You're not wrong," he said.

We awkwardly stared at each other for a moment, saying nothing.

"Well, it was nice meeting you, Madison. Hope you have a great day!" he said.

"You too! Thank you for helping me with the mess I created. I truly appreciate it," I said.

"No problem. Bye," he said.

"Bye," I said, smiling.

After that interaction, I went down the thriller aisle and browsed a few more books. Something about a good thriller makes for a great cozy night. Most of the thrillers I have read are such good page-turners that I always desperately want to know what happens next. After about fifteen minutes in that aisle, I decided to go and check out with only my self-help book. Hopefully, this can help me manage my emotions while I go through this process.

As I got to the checkout line, I couldn't help but notice that Benson was at the front of the line. For a second, he looked back and saw me in line and smiled at me. I smiled back. As the line got shorter, I saw him get a free bookmark from the counter but I tried to look away to avoid seeming like a creep. While looking at the cover of my book, I noticed someone standing in front of me. When I looked up, there he was.

"Here. I got you one of those free bookmarks. They're in a jar on the counter near the register, and for some reason, they're really high up. I thought you might like one," he said, handing me the bookmark.

"Thank you! That's so sweet of you," I said.

"You're welcome," he replied.

That was so sweet of him I thought. I immediately took the bookmark and placed it inside my book to avoid losing it. I watched him check out and leave the bookstore. I paid for my book and went outside to text my mom. Ten minutes later, I saw my mom park in a handicap parking space. I pushed myself, looking both ways, to the car. While getting in the car, my mom asked,

"Did you find anything good?"

"I did. I got a self-help book about overcoming adversity. Hopefully, I can get something out of it," I responded, showing her the book.

"I'm pretty sure you will. Let me see it. When you finish, can I borrow it? I'd love to read it too," she said, looking at the back of the book.

"Did you get my avocados?" I asked.

"I sure did! I got three of them. Some were a little too ripe, but I made sure to get the best ones. Do you have everything?” Mom asked, checking her purse.

“Pretty much,” I said, checking inside my crossbody bag to make sure I had my wallet. “Yeah, we’re good,” I reaffirmed.

# Chapter 5
## Secret Writing

Getting back to my new normal has been quite challenging. The hardest part has been grieving the moments I will never experience again in this lifetime. Everything feels heavy these days. Today, I feel like attempting to clean my bedroom. Maybe the process of tidying up my space will help me feel better. I started by dusting my dresser, where my record player sits.

For a moment, I reminisced about how deeply I once loved dancing. Dancing was a way for me to express myself. I felt a sense of freedom moving my body in ways that are now constricted. The thought of that freedom being part of my past haunts my mind. How is it possible that your life can change in a split second? I slowly opened my record player case and inserted my favorite vinyl, a copy of Beyoncé's Renaissance album. Listening to the beat automatically makes me feel alive again. Every lyric becomes a vibration that fills every inch of my body. No matter how dreadful life can be, music has always been there to cheer me up. Music is like a safety blanket I carry through the years. No matter how much time passes, the different tones and sounds always stay with me, becoming a part of who I am.

The music lifted my spirits and gave me the boost of energy I needed to tackle every task. I folded some laundry, changed my bedsheets, and threw away some old receipts that had been cluttering my drawers. Finishing these tasks felt like a huge accomplishment, especially now that it takes me a bit more time to do things I used to do with ease.

After my cleaning marathon, I decided to grab the book I purchased yesterday from the cute tote bag I got at the bookstore. I settled into my freshly washed, lavender-scented sheets to catch a glimpse of my new book. As I turned the paperback cover, I couldn't help but notice the bookmark that the guy at the library had given me. Looking at the bookmark, I suddenly saw that it had something written on the back.

*I think you're super cute. We should hang out sometime.*

*-Benson*

Below his name was his phone number.

"Wait, what? I didn't notice the writing on the back when he gave me the bookmark. I just

thought he was doing a good deed," I said aloud
to myself.

The thought of him instantly put a smile on
my face. "Should I text him?" I wondered.

Isn't it interesting how, when you least
expect it, people come into your life? I haven't
been feeling a hundred percent myself, and this
is the moment someone appears in my life. I set
the bookmark next to me and started to read the
first pages of the book.

After reading a few pages on the topic of
living in the now, I couldn't help getting
emotional.

For a second, I thought about Dylan. He was
such a beautiful human being, the way he lit up a
room just with his presence. Gosh, I miss him so
much.

He made everybody feel welcome. The thing I
admired most about him was his outlook on life.
He had a clear vision of what he wanted to do,
and now he's gone. I questioned myself over and
over again: did we really need to go out that
night? The guilt of him not being here doesn't
escape my mind. If it were my choice, he should
be the one living. He was full of life.

I closed my book and laid on my side, holding it close to my chest, and immediately started to cry. Crying feels like my only option these days. The saltiness of my tears occasionally cascading into my mouth is becoming a familiar taste. I just laid there, letting my emotions take control of my inner being.

A few hours have passed, and for some reason, I can't stop thinking about the guy from the bookstore. I wondered what he's up to. I can't believe that this guy, out of nowhere, has bumped into my life when I'm at my lowest. I grabbed the bookmark and looked at his phone number. "What am I going to say to him?" I wondered. I got a little nervous and started overthinking about what I should text him. I stared at my phone's keyboard for a few seconds, analyzing each conversation starter in my brain.

"Hi! It's Madison. The girl who fought for her life to get a self-help book off the shelf at Barnes & Noble. I found your secret writing on my bookmark," I typed.

A few minutes passed, and I instantly regretted sending the text. "Why did I say that? He's going to think I'm weird," I thought. I heard the messaging sound on my phone and got a little too excited to read the response.

"Hey! Hahaha. It wasn't supposed to be a secret, but I'm glad it caught your eye. You're very pretty. I thought I'd give it a shot," he responded.

"That was a first for me. I've never been approached like that before. Someone leaving their phone number and playing it cool like you did was very clever," I replied.

"Really?" he typed back.

"I'll give you credit for that. I would never have the courage to do something like that," I typed.

"At least it worked out in the end," he wrote.

"It definitely made me think of you, so I guess it did work out," I wrote.

"How old are you?" he asked.

"Twenty-two. And you?" I wrote.

"Twenty-four," he answered.

"Can I ask why you're in a wheelchair?" he inquired.

That question reminded me of how different my life is now. It's a question I've never had to answer before. I guess this is something I'll have to explain for the rest of my life. Reliving that traumatic event over and over again feels like reopening an old wound.

"A month ago, I got into a car accident with a friend that left me paralyzed from the waist down," I typed.

His response was noticeably slower this time.

"I'm so sorry to hear that. And how are you doing now?" he asked.

That's a question I haven't even asked myself, I thought.

"I'm alive. Struggling, but grateful to be alive," I replied.

And to think that I was bawling my eyes out just a few hours ago.

"I'm glad you're still here. I'm really glad we connected. I think you're pretty cool, if you ask me. I don't see you any differently than anyone else," he wrote.

"Thank you! I appreciate that. And what about you? What were you doing in the non-fiction aisle?" I typed.

"I was looking for something to help me get through life. I'm a bartender and have been struggling financially a bit. Reality has been weighing on me lately. I was searching for a 'get your life together' kind of book, but decided to save the day when I saw you struggling out of the corner of my eye," he replied.

"Hahaha. Thanks. That really made my day. The struggle was real. Who decides to put shelves that high when someone like me can't even reach seventy-five percent of those books?" I typed.

"You could ask someone for help," he typed.

"And what about accessibility?" I wrote.

"True. We should file a complaint," he replied.

"To who?" I asked.

"To the bookstore manager," he answered.

"You've got a point. I should start advocating for myself," I typed.

"Hey! I'm about to head out to my work shift. Do you mind if I text you tomorrow? I'd like to get to know you better, if you don't mind," he texted.

"I don't mind at all," I replied.

"Sweet! Talk to you tomorrow. Have a good night," he wrote.

"You too! Bye," I replied.

"Bye," he texted.

# Chapter 6
## Bad Days

Therapy can be quite challenging. Some days, I find myself making progress with my movements, and other days, I just want to give up. Today is one of those days. My physical therapist focused on my floor transfers. One thing I've learned from physical therapy is that each patient has their own personalized exercise plan. We all have different bodies and injuries, so it makes sense that each of us has different needs to address.

Transferring from the floor to my wheelchair as a paraplegic is something we have to work on, especially given the occasional falls from our wheelchairs that can occur from time to time. Today, I didn't feel like doing the same exercises over and over again. Lacking the upper body strength to push myself from the floor while positioning my non-working legs created such frustration within me. Shelby must be tired of hearing me say "ugh" over and over again. I tried multiple times until I finally gave up for the day. I felt like such a failure that I started to cry.

"That's OK. We can try another day. You gave it your all, and that's more than enough. We keep trying; that's all that matters," Shelby said.

When I heard those words, I put both of my hands over my face and wanted to hide from the world.

"Why are you upset? Do you want to talk about it?" Shelby asked, crouching next to me on the floor.

"I don't want to do this," I said, frustrated.

"The transfers? We can try another exercise if you want to," she suggested.

"I don't want to do any of this," I said, angry at myself.

"You don't have to do anything if you don't want to. I understand that this can be a difficult process, but you're not alone in this. We are here to assist and guide you on this journey," she said, making eye contact.

At that precise moment, I realized that I just wanted to go back to my old life. Looking back at everything, I hate that I took my body for granted. The freedom it provided me. How sometimes I didn't even care about nourishing it, and it still worked fine. Mourning that old version of me is mentally exhausting. Having self-compassion is something I'm struggling with right now. That's what inflicts pain on my soul. So I took a deep breath and felt the pressure start to subside. I decided to be present for a moment. Focusing on the now brought me peace and allowed me to compose myself. For the first time, I felt compassion for myself. Yesterday, I read that self-compassion can arise from your deepest pain. In that moment of frustration I tried to cherish my anguish.

My therapist helped me get off the floor and gave me a hug.

"As a friend, I want to see you doing the things you enjoyed before your accident. The things that gave you happiness. Those are the things that help us navigate these obstacles in life. Promise me that you're going to do more of that, whatever it is," she said, giving me a very meaningful hug.

I really thought about what Shelby said to me as I came home from therapy. It's the second time I've heard almost the same words from someone: get back to your life. I tried thinking of the things I used to love doing before being paralyzed, and taking care of our houseplants was one of them. My mom has these trillium plants in the backyard in a white round planter that I always used to take care of. In the spring, a three-leaf white flower blooms beautifully in contrast with their green leaves.

I went into the kitchen to grab a glass of water to replenish our decaying trilliums, and for a moment, I stayed outside just taking in the fresh air. The sound of tranquility that exudes from nature is music to my ears. For a moment, I thought about how every single organism just exists in perfect harmony with its surroundings. Maybe that's what I should focus my attention on: just existing. As I was watching some trees, I got a message from Benson.

"Hey! Been thinking about you all day. Do you want to go on a date this Saturday? I'm off this weekend," he texted.

"Hi! Go where?" I responded.

"Where would you like to go?" he asked.

"I don't know. I haven't thought of going out that much since all my focus has been on therapy these days," I replied.

"Let's go to the beach," he wrote.

"That's not going to be a great idea for my wheels. I'm probably going to get stuck in the sand," I wrote.

"There has to be a way. I got you. I can help you out if you need anything. It's going to be fun, and we could get to know each other better," he texted.

The thought of saying no instantly crossed my mind. All the "what ifs" of situations where I couldn't be part of the whole experience made me doubt if I should go or not. But having the conflicting thought of doing the things that I enjoyed doing came back to me, and I simply couldn't pass up the opportunity.

"Yeah! Sure," I replied.

"At what time do you want me to pick you up?" he asked.

"What about at ten-ish?" I suggested.

"Sure! I'll be there at that time. How was therapy?" he asked.

"Not good," I replied.

"Oh no. Why?" he asked.

"I wasn't feeling that great today. Everything I was doing wasn't working out. I don't think it was my day if I'm being honest," I answered.

"You can always try next time. We all have our bad days sometimes," he wrote.

"True. And what about you? How was your day?" I asked.

"I'm feeling a little bit tired. We were cleaning out the bar today. It was filthy! The amount of dirt that came from the floor was kind of gross now that I think about it, but overall, it was a great day," he replied.

I wish I was as happy as he sounds right now. Something about the way he views everything in such a positive way makes me curious if he is truly that happy all the time.

"You could have asked me to help. I love to clean—it's free therapy for me. You focus on the task, and it has a reward at the end of the day. I genuinely enjoy doing it," I wrote.

"Next time, I know who to call then. I'm excited to see you this weekend though," he wrote.

"Can't wait! Do you want me to bring something for the trip?" I asked.

"We could stop at the grocery store for some snacks if you want to?" he typed.

"We should. Sounds like a plan," I replied.

"See you Saturday then. Bring your self-help book that you picked from Barnes. I want to know your thoughts on it," he wrote.

"You remembered. Get ready to hear my live, laugh, love quotes that I annotated," I wrote.

"Oh, I can't wait. Have a good night!" he texted.

"You too!" I wrote.

# Chapter 7
## Life Isn't So Bad

Having dinner with my parents is my favorite part of the day. Tonight, we had mashed potatoes, oven-cooked chicken breast, and broccoli. This is the time we really get to sit down at the table and spend time with each other. If it weren't for my situation, I would probably be living on my own, missing these small moments with family.

Dad always has funny stories about his office clerk job. He went on a quick tangent about how the office printer wasn't working, and he had to hit the paper slot every second to get the paper unstuck with each use. I love seeing my mom laugh at his silly little hurdles. I admire their relationship so much that I hope to have one like theirs one day. My mom talked about how the kids in her classroom are all enjoying their reading time and contributing great critical thinking skills through the process of finding books they selected as a group.

"What about you, Madison? How did therapy go?" Dad asked.

"It's challenging, for sure," I said while circling my fork in my mashed potatoes. "I mean, I'm trying to make some progress, but for some reason, I feel like I'm not getting far enough."

"Give it time. That's why the process takes weeks. Don't get discouraged if something doesn't work out. We can always learn how to adapt to new things. If something doesn't work out, you can always find another way to do it," Dad said.

"Have you taken time to focus on other things besides therapy?" Mom asked.

"I have a date this Saturday," I said while eating a scoop of mashed potatoes.

"With who?" Dad asked, surprised.

His shock made me smile.

"A guy I met this past week at the bookstore," I said.

"Where are you guys going?" Mom asked.

"To the beach," I instantly replied.

"That sounds fun," Mom said, looking at Dad.

"How long have you been talking to him? I know this is none of my business, but you're recently adapting to your new life, and I don't want anyone taking advantage of you," Dad said, concerned about my date.

"Dad, what are you talking about? I'm twenty-two years old, not a teenager. He seems like a genuinely nice guy, and I met him at a bookstore. Do you really have to worry about a man who reads?" I said.

"You never know," Dad replied.

"I think going out and getting back out there is a great idea," Mom said.

I smiled at Dad, side-eyeing my mom.

"Just because she's now in a wheelchair, it doesn't mean she is going to be sheltered or closed off in a room," Mom said, looking directly at Dad. "I'm excited for you. Go out and have some fun," she added.

"She's right, but please be careful and call me immediately if something seems off," Dad said.

"Dad, I will. Don't worry about it. I'm going to be fine," I said.

"And you have a great point with the reading thing. At least he's educated. There are really dumb men out in the wild. You want to avoid that kind of man," he said jokingly.

We all laughed and finished our dinner. I helped Mom clear the table while Dad washed the dishes. For the rest of the night, I did my night routine, got into some comfy pajamas, and read a little. The thought of Benson made me fall asleep in a good headspace. Maybe life isn't that bad after all.

# Chapter 8
## Beach Day

It's 8:00 a.m., and I'm about to get ready for my date with Benson. I took a shower and went straight to the closet. "What am I going to wear? Maybe shorts?" I said to myself while looking through my pants drawer. I picked out some light-washed denim shorts. For my top, I chose a white sleeveless crop top, and since today's a little bit chilly, I added a light beige long-sleeve button-down, styled like a cardigan. I completed my outfit with a pair of white sneakers and a tote bag. And of course, I made sure to pack my book and some beach essentials in the tote. I quickly grabbed a rice cake with peanut butter on top before heading out the door.

Benson was waiting for me in the car. He stepped outside, and I couldn't help noticing how cute he looked. Who knew that a sweatshirt and some shorts could look so good on a man?

"Hi!" I said in a sweet tone that even surprised me.

"Hi," he answered, taking a look at my casual outfit. "You look good as always."

I blushed. "Thank you. You look good too," I said.

"Let me help you with your chair," Benson said, grabbing my tote bag.

He opened the door for me. I transferred from my wheelchair to the passenger seat and adjusted my legs. He leaned down and asked, "How do you take the wheels off?"

"There's a button in the center of the wheel. Just push it down, and they should come off easily," I said.

"Got it!" he said.

He was being so gentle with my chair. He took off both wheels and the seat, gently placing each part in the back seat. He handed me my tote bag and got inside the car.

"We got everything?" he asked.

"I think so," I replied.

"Let's stop at the grocery store really quick to grab some snacks," he said.

"Yeah, let's do that," I said. For some reason, I felt nervous. It's not the first time I have gone out with a guy, but something about Benson makes me feel something I can't even explain with words.

"What kind of music do you like listening to?" he asked.

"I usually listen to pop music. A lot of Dua Lipa, Gracie Abrams, Tate McRae, Chappell Roan, Beyoncé, and I could go on and on with my list for a whole day. I enjoy pretty much everything, I would say," I said, overthinking my response. "What about you?" I asked.

"I'm really into Noah Kahan right now, but I'm pretty much like you. I'm very open to hearing different genres of music," he said.

"Noah's music is so good. Have you heard of Hazlett?" I asked.

"No, I haven't," he said.

"He's an Australian indie-folk artist who is unbelievably good and so underrated. Let me put on a playlist. I'm pretty sure if you like Noah Kahan, you're going to love his music," I said, while looking for a playlist on Spotify.

"It's so cute how passionate you are about your music. We have to go to a concert together eventually and share the experience," he said.

"We should. What about you? What do you like to do for fun?" I asked.

"I really enjoy running or anything that has to do with the outdoors. I'm a very active person, and connecting with nature does wonders for my mind," he said.

"Can't relate," I said.

"About what?" he asked.

"About being out in nature. I'm literally an indoor cat, but it makes me really happy to know that you love the outdoors," I said.

"We should go camping one day," he said, while turning the car blinker on.

"Never," I said, teasing him.

"Come on! We can hike, make a bonfire, and even make some s'mores," he said.

"Hiking in a wheelchair?" I said, smiling.

"Sorry, that was stupid of me to say, but we can have a great time," he said.

"No, you're fine. Camping sounds like an adventure."

He smiled, and I smiled back at him. My nervousness subsided.

We arrived at our local grocery store. We grabbed some water bottles and browsed through the fresh produce aisle. I picked a Honeycrisp apple and some white grapes, and we both agreed on getting some corn tortilla chips with a guacamole dip. As we stood in the checkout line, a woman, probably in her eighties, approached me and said, "Excuse me, sweetheart. What a beautiful couple you two make."

"Oh no, we are just friends, but that is so kind of you to say," I said.

"Oh dear, I'm so sorry. Anyways, you look beautiful together as friends too," she said.

I smiled at her endearing approach. I offered to let her go ahead of us since we only had a few items.

"That is so nice of you. Have a great day, sweetie!" she said.

"You too," I said.

We took our snacks to the car and headed straight to the beach. When we arrived, I couldn't help but stare at the beauty of nature. Where the sky meets the ocean, you can see the different hues of blue that instantly take your breath away. The cream-colored sand hugs the final stage of each wave, creating a beautiful ocean sound. Patches of weeds add a splash of color to the neutral tones of the sand. On top of the weeds, the pampas grass moves in the direction of the cool ocean breeze. Something about seeing the ocean makes me feel so small. Seeing nature in its fullest form makes your problems seem insignificant. Benson helped me with my chair, and we walked through a wooden pier that led to the sand.

"Do you want to sit on the sand?" Benson asked, his eyes sparkling with enthusiasm.

"I don't think I could get my wheelchair through it," I replied, glancing at the uneven surface.

"I'll carry you. We'll figure it out," he said with a determined smile.

"But how?" I asked, feeling a mix of excitement and nervousness.

"Piggyback. Let me take our stuff down there first, and then I'll come back for you," he said, already moving towards the beach.

As I watched him set up our things on the sand, a wave of gratitude washed over me. Being here with him made me forget all the struggles I'd been facing recently. The effort he was putting in to make me comfortable made me feel truly appreciated.

"Ready!" he called out. "Put your arms around my neck and hold on tight. I'm going to grab your legs and lift you up. Trust me, I won't let you fall."

So I did. I trusted him, a stranger. Trust was something I struggled with, but in order to get closer to people, I knew I had to let my guard down. I always kept my walls up, but something about Benson made me feel comfortable. He felt like home. So I completely trusted him.

"See? It wasn't that bad," he said as I held on, my legs wrapped around his waist.

"Imagine if we both face-planted in the sand right now," I said, laughing.

"Don't make me laugh, or I might lose my strength," he replied, trying to stifle his laughter.

"Okay, Superman," I teased.

We both laughed lightly, though we were genuinely concerned we might tumble into the sand at any moment.

"There we go. I'm going to slowly put you down on the sand," he said.

And he did. The landing was a bit rough, but we made it. He went back to get my chair from the pier and then sat next to me.

"There goes your upper body workout for the day. Let me get you a water bottle," I said, reaching into my tote bag.

We both stared at the ocean for a moment, enjoying the peaceful sound of the waves.

"Tell me more about you," I said, breaking the silence.

"What do you want to know?" he asked.

"How's your relationship with your family?" I asked.

"Umm, not great. I haven't talked to my parents in about two years now," Benson said, his tone shifting.

"Why?" I asked gently.

"Family stuff," he answered, the weight of his words hanging in the air.

"You don't have to talk about it if you don't want to," I said, not wanting to press him.

"Growing up, my parents fought a lot. Not physically, but they argued constantly. They despised each other. I never understood how they got married in the first place. So yeah, I grew up in a very dysfunctional household," he said.

"I'm sorry to hear that. Do you have any siblings?" I asked.

"I have an older brother. He lives in Colorado with his wife and kids," Benson said.

"And do you guys get along?" I asked.

"We keep in touch. I don't see him often, but we have a good relationship," he said, looking at the ocean. "What about you? How's your relationship with your parents?"

"We're very close. Sometimes I forget to be grateful for having such great parents," I said.

"Do you have any siblings?" he asked.

"No, it's just me. I always wanted to have a sister, though," I said.

"Growing up as an only child must be lonely," he said.

"It was. I was constantly playing by myself. Maybe that's why I grew up to love my alone time," I said.

There was a brief silence.

"Why are you single?" I asked.

"What do you mean by why?" he asked, raising an eyebrow.

"Okay, that came out wrong. When was your last relationship?" I asked, correcting myself.

"A year ago," he said.

"Why did it end? I'm sorry if I'm being too nosy. It feels like I'm interrogating you," I said, apologetically.

"No, you're good. We're getting deep. I like that," he said. "Now that I think about it, we had different views on life. She wanted to get married, and I didn't. We were so young, and I felt like I still hadn't figured out what I wanted in life. I'm still not stable enough to make that jump. I want to make sure that when I get married, it feels right."

"What about you?" he asked.

"Oh, I've only been in one relationship, and it was in high school. Relationships haven't been my focus. I've always been more driven by my goals and dreams," I said.

"You can have someone by your side during that process, don't you think?" he asked.

"I know, but I'm an all-or-nothing kind of person. Maybe I need to balance things out. Maybe you're right. I need to work on that," I admitted.

"And what are those dreams and goals?" Benson asked.

"Well, I'm in college studying something that doesn't align with any of them," I said.

"What are you majoring in?"

"Accounting. As someone who loves all things creative," I said.

"Hey! You can color-code your spreadsheets," he said, grinning.

I laughed. "I can make them colorful to fulfill my creative dreams," I said, smiling. "But no, I'm still trying to figure life out."

"What about you? Do you have any dreams or aspirations?" I asked.

"I would love to go to college and study psychology. That's always been a passion of mine. Hopefully, I get to do it one day," he said.

"So you love helping people," I said.

"Pretty much. I think I'm a good listener. I want to be part of something that makes the world a better place. What better way than listening and guiding people through their feelings?" he said.

"That's amazing. I'm sure you'll accomplish it. You have a good purpose," I said.

"Did you bring your book?" he asked.

"Yes, I did," I said, reaching into my tote bag.

"The last chapter I read talked about how your past doesn't define your present or your future. It's the now that matters. I really enjoyed it," I said.

"Take it. Read it and let me know if you love it as much as I did," I said, handing him the book.

He flipped through a few pages.

"This is the kind of book I usually enjoy. I feel like I learn a lot from non-fiction. I'll give you my thoughts on it and hand it back to you when I finish," he said.

"I think you're going to love it then," I said. "It really delves deep into our negative thought patterns and provides excellent advice on how to navigate adversity."

We sat in the sand, the sun casting a warm glow over the beach as the waves gently lapping at the shore. I glanced over at Benson, his eyes reflecting the shimmering ocean.

We shared laughs and exchanged stories, each one more interesting than the last. Minutes turned into hours as we focused on the now, enjoying each other's company. I reached into the bag between us and pulled out a container of chips and guacamole. "Hungry?" I offered.

"Absolutely," he replied, taking a chip and dipping it generously. "You know, there's something magical about eating on the beach. Everything tastes better."

We savored the salty chips and creamy guacamole, talking about our favorite foods and best beach memories. At one point, Benson picked up a seashell and handed it to me. "This one's for you. A little souvenir from today."

"Thanks," I said, examining the intricate patterns on the shell. "It's beautiful."

As the sun began to set, painting the sky in hues of orange and pink, we decided to build a sandcastle. Laughing like kids, we dug and molded the sand, adding shells and stones for decoration.

Eventually, the air grew cooler, and I knew it was time to head back. I started gathering our things, shaking off the sand and packing up our snacks. Benson helped, and as we finished up, he looked at me with a smile. We headed back to my house.

"We should hang out sometime soon," Ben said as I was grabbing my things from the car.

"We should. I would love that. I had a great time with you today," I replied, smiling.

"Me too," he said, and before I could react, he leaned in and gave me a kiss on the cheek.

"Talk to you later," he added.

"Bye!" I said, feeling a warmth spread through me as I watched him drive away.

As I rolled up to the front door, my mom suddenly opened it, her eyes sparkling with excitement.

"How was it?" she asked eagerly.

"Were you peeking through the window this whole time?" I teased.

"No, I was just looking to see who parked their car in our driveway. That was a lie, maybe a little bit. I was really curious. He's so handsome,

Maddie. From what I saw from afar," she admitted with a mischievous grin.

"Mom, you can't be doing that," I said, shaking my head.

"I was just looking. What's wrong with that?" she said defensively.

"It was fun. I had a great time with him," I said, trying to deflect her curiosity.

"Do you like him?" she asked, her eyes searching mine.

"He's a nice guy. I don't know him that well to say that. Time will tell," I said, entering through the front door.

"Are you hungry? I made salmon with white rice," she said, changing the subject.

"I am. A little bit," I admitted.

"Let me serve you a plate," she said, heading straight to the kitchen.

Tonight, I couldn't stop thinking about Benson. My mom's question echoed in my mind: "Do you like him?" I really think so, I thought. When I was with him today at the beach,

everything felt right. Not for a second did I doubt
that I was with the right person at the right time.
He's truly becoming someone I want to get to
know better. For now, everything looks
picture-perfect in my head.

# Chapter 9
## Life Choices

I have my laptop sitting in front of me. I'm sitting at my dining room table, questioning for the hundredth time whether I'm making the right decision. I nervously click the withdrawal icon for my four classes. That's it; there's no turning back.

I feel so lost. I'm depressed and anxious all the time. Dealing with grief while adapting to my whole new world has not been easy. It's time for me to figure out what I truly want in life. Being so close to death made me realize that life is too short not to focus on the things we really love to do. My heart was never in becoming an accountant. The societal pressure to have a successful career got to me. I need to figure out for myself what success really means to me. I don't know what's next for me, but deep down, I knew this was the right choice. I closed my laptop and took a deep breath.

My emotions go up and down these days. It's interesting how, when you experience a traumatic event in your life, everything around you keeps moving forward. My life just stopped for an instant, and I have to cope with the aftermath while trying to keep up with everything else. It's like life never lets you catch a breath.

I feel nervous all of a sudden, and small tears accumulate on my lashes. There's not a single day that I don't think about Dylan and his family. I can't imagine how his parents must be feeling. It truly breaks my heart every time I think about them. I'm so frustrated that I can't go back in time and change everything. I closed my eyes and started to focus on my breathing. I inhale and exhale slowly. I can feel my chest loosening with each breath. I opened my eyes and took my bowl of oatmeal to the kitchen to clean up. While unloading the dishwasher, I hear a text message on my phone.

"Good morning, sunshine," Ben texted.

"Hi!" I responded.

"What are you doing?" he asked.

"Just finished unloading the dishwasher. What about you?" I wrote.

"I'm about to hop in the shower. I went for my morning run and couldn't stop thinking about you," he said.

"Ben!" I said.

"What? It's true," he said.

"You are making me like you a little bit more," I wrote.

"What? You don't like me?" he asked.

"I think you're pretty cool," I responded.

"Not what I wanted to hear, but I'll take it," he said.

"Thank you for making me feel better. I've been feeling down lately," I wrote.

"Talk to me," he said.

"I just dropped all my classes for this semester, and I have been feeling upset if I'm being honest. There's too much going on in my head," I said.

"Can't imagine what you are going through. Take your time. Don't overthink it. Everything is going to be alright. I wish I could give you a hug right now," he wrote back.

"Thank you!" I said.

"Do you want to go out tonight for some drinks? There's a new bar in town that recently opened, and I want to check it out. They're going to have live music. Do you want to go?" he asked.

"I do love live music. Let's be honest; if there's music, you know that I'm going to be there," I texted.

"Say less. I'll pick you up at six," he said.

"Sounds like a plan," I said.

"See you then," he wrote.

"Thank you for lifting my mood. Just wanted to let you know that I appreciate you so much," I wrote.

"So that means you like me a little?" he said.

"See you at six!" I responded.

It was 7:21 p.m., and we arrived at The Rusty Nail bar. The outside of the venue looked like a European building. The structure was all painted black with arched windows all over the front. Every wall was adorned with intricate wall molding that instantly transported you to the east part of the world. These huge cast-iron black wall lamps illuminated the outdoor concrete sidewalk. The bar had a moody, almost castle-like look to it. Inside, reddish-brown brick covered most of the interior walls. Rustic black pendant lights with Edison bulbs created cozy ambient lighting. Rich dark wood tones were used on the floor, bar, chairs, and tables.

"Wow, this place is beautiful," I said to Ben as we walked through the bar entrance.

"I know, right? Where do you want to sit?" he said in my ear. The music was a little loud.

"Let's do the tables in the corner," I said back close to his ear.

We sat down, and the first thing I saw in the corner was a live artist singing country music. They had a small stage in the center and an open space so people could dance.

"Welcome! What can I get for you tonight?" the waiter said with a tablet in her hand.

The menu was sitting on top of our table.

"Hi!" we both said,

"Umm. Let me see," I said as I took a quick look at the menu.

"I'm going to let you take a look at the menu, and whenever you're ready, let me know. My name is Katie if you need anything," she said.

"Thank you," we both responded.

"What are you in the mood for?" Ben said.

"I don't have anything specific in mind," I said as I looked down at the appetizers section. "What about you?" I asked.

"The specialty cheeseburger with caramelized onions sounds good to me," he said.

"That sounds really good. I think I'm going to get the bruschetta topped with tomatoes, basil, and olive oil," I said.

"Nice! It sounds fancy when you say it like that," he said.

"It does sound fancy when it's just toasted bread," I said, smiling. "You look nice today. The black button-down shirt makes your eyes pop," I said.

"Thank you, so do you. As always, of course. I like the shiny fabric," he said, looking at my dress.

"Shiny fabric? You mean satin," I said.

"Yeah, that's what I was trying to say," he said, embarrassed.

We both laughed.

"Anyway, you look really pretty today," he said, making eye contact.

"Thank you, so do you. You look very handsome," I said, staring back at him.

"Are you guys ready to order?" Katie asked.

"Yeah, can we get an order of the specialty cheeseburger, please? And an order of the bruschetta," I said.

"And to drink?" Katie asked.

"Two beers, please," Ben replied.

"We have a specialty burger, an order of bruschetta, and two beers. Correct? Anything else I can get for you?" Katie asked.

"No, that would be all," I said.

"I'm going to leave you the order number here. If you need anything, let me know," Katie said.

"Thank you!" We both replied.

Our eyes met as we smiled at each other. Sometimes you don't have to say anything to express how you feel about someone. When you have a bond with another person, just being by their side is enough to appreciate the silence.

"We haven't talked about what you're looking for in a girlfriend," I said to break the silence.

"That's a great question. I haven't thought much about it, to be honest. I guess I want someone I can share my life with, someone I can see a future with. What about you?" he said.

"I see myself with someone who truly loves me for who I am. Someone honest. Someone who will be by my side not only in the good moments of life but in the moments when everything feels like it's falling apart. That's the kind of love I want," I said. "Do you see yourself getting married one day?"

"When the right person comes and when it feels right. Absolutely. Do you see yourself getting married one day?" he said.

"Yeah. Not only that, I would love to be a mom one day," I said.

"How many kids would you like to have?" he asked.

"More than one. Being an only child can be lonely, especially when growing up. Two or three. Do you see yourself becoming a father?" I said.

"Hopefully. I would love to have the healthy family dynamic that I never experienced growing up," he said. "So when are we getting married?"

"Tomorrow. No, I'm just kidding," I said, smiling.

Just in time, the food arrived. Eating while hearing live music was a fun experience. The bruschetta tasted like it was freshly made. The bread was crispy enough on the sides, and the mixture of tomato and olive oil made me think I was in Italy for a brief moment. After we finished our delicious dinner, Ben suggested that we go to the dance floor.

"I don't think that's a great idea," I said.

"Why not?" Ben asked.

"I could stumble into half of the people there," I said. "And besides, I don't want to be stared at the whole time." I said, glancing at the small crowd of people.

"Be stared at for what? You are allowed to have fun. Who cares? I'm going to be by your side," he said, standing up from his chair. "Come on. Lose yourself a little. Let's have some fun."

"Ben, I really think..." I tried to say as he walked in front of me, waiting for me to follow him.

I gave up and followed him to the dance floor. The funny thing is, I wouldn't hesitate when Dylan and I used to go dancing on our night adventures. Now I feel self-conscious about every single part of my body. Dua Lipa's "Levitating" was blasting on the speaker. Ben started doing some dance moves that instantly made me laugh. He took one of my hands and spun me around. At that point, I gave up my resistance and joined in. Everything I used to feel when I went out before my accident came back to me. I let loose and enjoyed the moment. I felt free, and my fear of judgment slowly went away. I'm glad I got out of my comfort zone and stayed present enough to celebrate just being alive.

After a few dance numbers, we went back to our table. As we were walking down the hallway, a young guy stopped us.

"Hey! Hey! Hey! Do you have a license for that thing?" he said.

He instantly made me uncomfortable.

"You are too beautiful to be in a wheelchair," he said as he gently touched my face. He was clearly intoxicated. I could smell the alcohol from miles away.

"Hey! Can you not?" Ben said.

"What's up, buddy! Is this your boyfriend?" he said, looking in my direction. "Damn, pretty enough to have a boyfriend already," he said.

At this point, Ben stepped in front of me, facing the guy directly.

"Can you leave her alone?" Ben said, making eye contact with the stranger.

"What are you going to do, buddy? I see you going for the low-hanging fruit," he said.

"Why don't you fuck off?" Ben said.

"Come at me, bro. If you are such a man," he said, patting his chest like he's some sort of animal.

The guy pushed Ben with extreme force. Ben almost got knocked down. He regained his composure and punched the guy, and they both started to fight.

"Stop! Stop! Stop!" I yelled as a group of people gathered around to separate them.

"Bitch! You are lucky we were not outside," he said.

"Yeah! Sure. Fucking loser," Ben responded.

The manager approached us and said that we had to get out of the bar. As we got outside, the guy kept insulting us from the sidewalk.

"Hey! Your disabled girlfriend is not even a full-ass woman. Good luck hitting that!" The guy said from the street while his friends tried to stop him as he tried to get closer to us.

"Dude, you want to fucking walk home with a few teeth missing?" Ben yelled with a tone of voice full of anger that I had never heard before.

"No, Ben, stop. Please, it's not necessary. Let him go. He's not worth your time," I said, scared that they might get into another altercation.

We kept walking in the opposite direction of the guy. Ben was still agitated from the confrontation. The whole situation made me really upset and guilty about everything. I think it was a mistake to come to a place where stuff like this can happen. I should've known better.

"I'm so sorry, Ben," I said.

"Sorry for what?" he said, trying to calm down.

"For everything that just happened." I said, as I noticed that blood was dripping down his nose. "Your nose is bleeding. Let me get you a tissue." As I grabbed a tissue from my purse, Ben stopped and sat down at the curb.

"You don't need to apologize. You didn't do anything," he said as he wiped his nose. "People are just hateful for no fucking reason."

"Does it hurt?" I asked, concerned about his nose.

"Nah, I'm fine. Hey, at least I saw you having fun on the dance floor. That's all that matters. Don't let people take that from you," he said.

"I loved every second of it," I said.

"See! It was all worth it. And the hurtful shit that douchebag said means nothing. He clearly doesn't know anything about you. I don't see you as any less than someone standing or sitting down. I see you for who you are. I would never let someone disrespect you like that," he said, looking directly into my eyes.

What he said triggered something in my soul and immediately brought tears to my eyes. The helplessness combined with the anxiety of everything that just went down got to me.

"You don't have to cry. It's fine. We are fine," he said while giving me a hug. Time stood still for a few seconds. "Let's go home," he said, giving me a kiss on the cheek.

The streets at 11:00 p.m. on a Sunday night were completely desolate. In every corner, there was not a single soul in sight. I couldn't help but get anxious as the stillness of the road reminded me of that terrible night. Every memory from that night with Dylan replayed in my head like a broken cassette. The harder I tried to shut down my last moments with him, the more I was reminded of what his last breath felt like.

"Are you okay?" Ben asked.

The question made my head shake. "Yeah. I'm fine. Why?" I replied.

"You seem a little off," he said.

"It must be that I'm tired," I said.

"You can close your eyes for a while. We are like twenty minutes away," he said.

"No, I'm okay," I said.

"Are you sure?" he said.

"Yes. Two sets of eyes on the road are safer than one," I said.

He looked at me and gave me a gentle smile. We safely made it home. I took my seat belt off and immediately went for a hug. Something in me made me give him the tightest hug. My feelings for him are growing each time I get to be with him. He's the sweetest, most caring, and genuine man I have ever met. I'm falling for him so hard. I can totally see a future with him in it. I gave him a kiss on the cheek.

"Make sure you text me when you get home," I said, looking straight into his eyes.

"I will. Let me help you out," he said.

## Chapter 10
## Unleashing My Inner Artist

I faintly heard knocking on my bedroom door.

"Maddie! Madison! Can I come in?" Mom called.

"The door is open!" I said, rubbing my eyes.

"Look what I got!" Mom said with a bright smile on her face. "When I was at the grocery store, there were some young people giving away flyers for a new art studio that's opening in the shopping plaza, and I instantly thought of you," Mom added as she sat at the end of the bed.

"I don't think I'm that great at painting," I said.

"Who says you have to be good at something to try it out? You've always had an inclination for anything creative. Why not give it a shot?" she said.

I took the flyer, squinted my eyes, and read it.

Canvas Dreams Studio

Art Workshop

Every Wednesday

6:00 p.m. - 7:30 p.m.
178 Tropical Island Shopping Plaza
North Carolina, ST 432

**Come Unleash Your Inner Artist!**
**Paint Supplies provided with initial $50 payment**

"I don't have the money to do it right now," I said, staring at the flyer.

"Don't worry about it. I'll pay for it. Who knows? Maybe you will end up loving it," she said. "How was your date with Benson?"

"It was fun until he got into an altercation with a guy who was excessively drunk," I said.

"Really! Oh my god. Is he okay?" she asked, concerned.

"He has a few bruises on his face and a bloody nose. Thankfully, nothing major," I replied.

"Over what?" she asked.

"The guy was being an overall jerk. He was just rude and provoking us for no reason," I said.

I didn't want to tell my mom the whole story. Between everything that we've been through, I don't want her to worry about something else.

"Maddie, please be careful when you go out. Things are not like they used to be back in the day," she said.

"I know. I promise you I'm going to try my best not to put myself in these situations," I said. "I'm excited to see if this painting class sparks my creativity. I think the more I put my energy into something, the better I'm going to feel," I said, looking at the flyer. "Thank you for thinking of me," I added, giving my mom a hug.

"You're welcome! Now it's time to get up. I've already done three things on my to-do list for the day, and you haven't even gotten out of bed," she said as she got up.

There was a line of about fifteen people for the art workshop. People of all ages seemed interested in the class, from those my age to those in their sixties. As we walked inside the art studio, there was a lot of empty floor space. Polished concrete floors filled the entire space with a light hue of gray. The open concept reminded me of a warehouse, but on a smaller scale. There was a wall full of glass that looked over the parking lot. Six tables were in the middle of the room, each with multiple chairs on each side facing the instructor.

"Good evening, everyone! Please grab a seat wherever you feel comfortable. You can pick from the left or the right tables. Your choice!" he said.

I chose to sit on the right side near the glass windows in the first row.

"Let me make some space and move this chair so you can sit comfortably," the instructor said.

"Thanks!" I replied.

"You're more than welcome," he said with a smile.

"Are we all situated?" he asked, looking across the room. "Okay, perfect! Hi everyone! My name is Alex. I'm going to be your art instructor for the next few weeks. Hopefully, you all stick around for the complete workshop. I'm so excited to embark on this new journey with all of you, and my goal is to teach you how to communicate your creativity through art. First and foremost, I would like each of you to introduce yourself to your fellow colleagues so we can get to know each other better. Please say your name out loud and what your expectations are for this workshop. We'll start from this side," he said, extending his hand toward my table.

"Hi! My name is Emily. My expectation for this class is to learn new painting techniques. I have been painting for about a year and a half alone at home, but I wanted to learn from someone with more experience and improve my skills," she said out loud.

"Welcome, Emily! I'm excited that you seem very passionate about art. I'm sure you'll learn a lot and gain the new skills you're looking for. Thank you for being here," Alex said.

Next, it was my turn. I don't know why group introductions make me so anxious. I hate the feeling of hearing my own voice in a sea of silence.

"What about you?" Alex asked.

"Hi everyone! My name is Madison." I had to resist the temptation to say that I'm here because I'm more lost than ever, but thankfully I had some self-control. "My expectation for this workshop is to find a way to express my creativity. I'm a very creative person, and painting is something I've always wanted to try," I said out loud.

"Did that make any sense?" I thought. My brain went blank for a minute.

"Welcome, Madison! I can't wait for you to explore this new venture. I'm very optimistic that you're going to love it. Thank you for being here," he said.

Each individual introduced themselves one by one. There were thirteen people in total.

"Again, thank you all for being here. During this process, make sure you get to know your colleagues. Collaboration is key in our everyday life. You can learn a lot from your peers as I guide you through this process. We are all here to learn, including me. For your first task, I want you to convey your feelings into a painting. How have you been feeling these past few days? Let the answer to that question guide you through your process. I want you to be vulnerable and let all those feelings out. Make this moment a time to reflect on your life. Be bold and don't hold back. Paint supplies are provided in the cabinets behind you. So let's get to work, and most importantly, let's have some fun," he said, putting both hands together.

At the back of the studio, the cabinets were full of art supplies. Every single item was neatly organized, looking like something out of a craft store. I grabbed a small canvas, a set of brushes, a container of water, and a box of oil paints that included ten tubes of primary and secondary colors, along with black and white.

At first, I didn't have a clue what I wanted to paint, so I mixed some colors to create a beautiful shade of light purple and proceeded to paint the entire canvas that color. The thought of flowers came to mind, so I started to paint a bouquet of flowers in a round white vase.

Minutes felt like milliseconds. With each brushstroke, the thoughts of everyday life disappeared. I was more focused than ever on finishing the painting. Without even noticing, our time was up for the day. Alex wanted to see our progress and give us some feedback before we left. He went around and had a conversation with each of us.

"Madison, right? If I remember correctly," he said.

"Yes!" I replied.

"Tell me more about your painting?" he asked as he stood next to me.

"My idea was to paint daisies in a flower vase. Half of the daisies are dying because I wanted to portray how life can be both beautiful and heartbreaking at the same time. I wanted to show how there can be beauty in pain. Life sometimes shows us two sides of the coin, the good and the bad. It's up to us to decide which side to focus on. That's what's been on my mind these days," I said, proud of my interpretation.

"I like that. Powerful statement," he said.

He leaned down to my eye level, and I couldn't help but notice his freckles and piercing blue eyes. His red hair and perfectly trimmed beard framed his defined jawline. His gray knitted sweater and pair of skinny trim silver glasses made him look like the stereotype of a professor you usually see in movies.

"Your shading needs more work. Let me borrow your brush. If you spend more time blending the edges, it will make them look more realistic," he said. "Try it."

So I did. I moved my brush similarly to how I blend my eyeshadow makeup.

"See the difference? Much, much better. Overall, great job," he said.

He took the time to give feedback to each one of us. "Okay class, gather around! That's going to be all for today. It was a pleasure getting to know each of you. You are a very talented group. Most importantly, I hope you felt inspired today and want to come back for our next session. Again, thank you for being part of this workshop. Give yourselves a round of applause," he said while clapping.

"Have a great rest of your night and see you next Wednesday," he said.

I waited outside the studio until my mom arrived to pick me up.

"How was it?" she asked.

"Better than I imagined. It was so much fun. I think this is something I could see myself taking seriously," I responded, feeling happy that I got out of my comfort zone and tried something new.

"Ahh, I'm so happy to hear that. I knew you would love it," she said.

# Chapter 11
## Stargazing

"Hey! Did you make it home?" I said over the phone.

"Hi! No, I'm actually five minutes away from my apartment. What are you up to?" Ben said.

"Last night I was doing some research online and found a campground that looks decently accessible. Should we go on a weekend trip?" I said, staring out my bedroom window.

"Nah. Really? I thought you said you hated camping," he said.

"Kind of, but it doesn't hurt to get out of my comfort zone," I said.

"Did you make the site reservation?" he asked.

"No, I was waiting for your thoughts on the idea," I responded.

"Let's do it. I'm excited," he said.

The weekend came around, and as Benson drove, I stared out the car window, seeing longleaf pine trees for miles. Trees big enough that created a beautiful shadow on the street. The vibrant lime green grass mixed with several patches of dirt made the scenery look straight out of a painting. It was a clear blue sky kind of day. As we arrived at the campground, there was a sign made out of logs that read Pine Ridge Campground.

"We arrived!" Benson said.

Ben parked his car at our booked site, which had a densely packed gravel path. Each site spot had a number carved into a wood plank nailed to a tree. There was a black picnic table to our left, snuggled between three pine trees. Next to it was a round fire pit made out of rocks.

"What do we do now?" I said as we got out of the car.

"Do you want to help me with the tent?" he asked.

"Sure. I don't know if I'll be a huge help, but you can tell me what to do," I said.

Ben took the tent out of the box and handed me a few poles.

"Help me connect them together so we can drape the tent over the frame," he said.

"Got it," I said, concentrating on connecting the poles for a few minutes.

I looked over to Ben, who was stretching the tent over the ground.

"Done. Now what?" I said.

"Let me connect them all together to create the structure," he said.

As he tried to connect and stretch the poles, they kept falling apart.

"Did I connect them wrong?" I asked.

"No, they are fine," he said, frustrated.

He was trying so hard, but it kept falling and falling. At first, I was serious, but after a few failed attempts and reassuring him of how I could help, it honestly made me laugh.

"What are you laughing at?" he asked.

"I thought you had camping experience?" I said.

"Hey! I've been doing this since I was a little kid," he said, still struggling to get the poles to stand up.

"Are you sure? It doesn't look like it," I said, laughing.

"You laughing doesn't help either," he said.

"Do you think it will be up before tomorrow?" I asked.

"Can you imagine me being here all night? That would be hilarious, I'm not going to lie," he said.

"Should we find a tutorial on YouTube?" I asked.

"No, we are good. There! See! It just needed a little love. Now we drape the fabric all over and secure the four corners, and we're done," he said.

When he finished building the tent, he was all sweaty and exhausted. I checked my phone, and it was an eighty-one-degree day in May.

"Let's get you some water," I said.

We brought two reusable insulated water bottles and an extra canister that we could fill up at the campground's bathroom if we ran out of water. We grabbed the bottles from the trunk of Ben's car and sat at the picnic table.

"Did you go camping a lot growing up?" I asked.

"Every two or three weeks with my brother and dad during the late spring and summer seasons. I looked forward to it every single time. It was my favorite part of my childhood, if I'm being honest," he said.

"What do you like most about it?" I asked, genuinely interested.

"Everything. Especially the peace and quiet of nature. I bonded a lot with my brother too. We used to play with the pine sticks and pretend they were magical swords or wands. It was definitely the good old days," he said, taking a drink from his water bottle.

"What about you? What did you do for fun growing up?" he asked.

"I used to read a lot and play with my dolls. We didn't take many vacations growing up. We didn't have a lot of money, so we usually stayed home for the summer. As an only child, I didn't have anyone to play with, so I really got into books and playing pretend with my dolls," I said.

"What kind of person were you in high school?" I asked.

"I was into sports. I used to do cross-country," he said.

"The jock," I said.

"Pretty much, but I did well in school. I was a straight-A student while I focused on my cross-country running," he said.

"And let me guess, you were part of the popular kids?" he asked.

"No, absolutely not. I was far from popular. I was the shy and reserved girl in my class. I was teased a lot for it. It was just me and my books. A young and naive bookworm," I said, half-smiling, slowly spinning my water bottle.

"Look at you now. You are a very cute and pretty cool girl, if you ask me," he said.

"Thanks," I said, smiling and looking into his eyes.

"Do you think we would be friends if we had met in high school?" I asked.

"Yeah. A thousand percent. Girlfriend and boyfriend actually. High school sweethearts for sure," he said confidently.

I blushed.

"You'd probably be more interested in the popular girls," I said, teasing him.

"I don't think so," he said.

We smiled at each other.

"Do you want to help me get the rest of the things from the car?" he asked.

"Yeah. We can set up everything here on the table for now," I said.

We brought three grocery bags, some pre-sliced watermelon, and pre-made chicken wraps from the grocery store. Mostly snacks and a bag of marshmallows, some chocolate, and graham crackers to make s'mores. We opened the container of watermelon and stared at our surroundings. We could hear birds chirping in the trees. The wind navigated its way through the branches. The sound of nature kept us distracted, with no need to check our phones.

"You never told me exactly how your accident happened," he said.

"So basically, I went to a music festival with my best friend, and on our way back home, someone got in the middle of our lane. My best friend steered the car out of the way, and we ended up hitting a tree. Sadly, Dylan didn't make it," I said.

When I talk about Dylan, I always get a knot in my throat. No matter how much time passes, it always affects me.

"I'm sorry to hear that," he said.

"That's okay. I'm still here, and that's all that matters," I said, taking a sip of water as I tried to push those memories aside.

"What about you? Have you experienced something that has changed your life forever?" I asked.

"Besides meeting you," he said.

He instantly made me feel better.

"No, I would say not seeing my parents have a normal, loving relationship affected me a lot. I didn't grow up in a stable home. We lived surrounded by chaos. It was hard to accept that the people who one day decided to be together because they were in love ended up hating each other. On a few occasions, I blamed myself, thinking it was my fault they acted the way they did, and I questioned my existence many times. I know it affected my brother too. Everything we experienced shaped the person I am today," he said.

"I'm sorry that you had to go through all that," I said.

"That's okay. I guess we are all dealing with something in life. So yeah." He looked off into the distance. "Do you want to go on a walk?" he asked.

"Yeah, let's go," I said.

We walked along a fairly flat hiking trail, surrounded by pine trees on either side. Other people were also walking the same path. Although the path was a bit bumpy, I managed to maneuver my chair. My chair got stuck in the dried dirt a few times, but Ben helped me out.

We kept going until we found a log where Ben
wanted to sit.

"Look at the cute squirrel," I said.

"You mean the furry rat?" he asked.

"Ben, that's so mean," I teased him.

"What? They're considered rodents. It
probably has a long-lost cousin roaming the
streets of New York," he said, staring at the
squirrel.

"Oh no, you scared it away," I said, pretending
to be sad like a child.

"It probably got offended," he said, laughing.

Ben looked at the sky. "It looks like it's going
to rain. Should we go back?" he asked.

"We should," I said.

As we walked back, it started to get really
cloudy. The gloomy gray sky was a clear sign that
rain was imminent. And it did. At first, we tried to
walk faster to avoid getting drenched, but we
quickly realized that we would be completely
soaked by the time we reached our campsite
anyway. The sound of raindrops hitting the trees

and grass was incredibly relaxing. The cold rain hit our faces as we moved forward. We both wondered why we were rushing when we knew we'd end up completely wet anyway. So, we took our time. The rain reminded me that even on our darkest days, there is still beauty to be found. Nature doesn't hurry because it rains; it embraces it. And that's what we did.

"Did you play in the rain when you were little?" I asked.

"All the time. That was one of the best parts of being a kid. Playing in the rain with neighborhood friends is something I actually miss from my childhood," he said.

"Me too. And to think I wanted to grow up so quickly, only to realize that being an adult isn't that fun," I said, raindrops getting in my eyes.

"Being an adult doesn't have to be boring. We have other forms of entertainment," he said.

"Like what?" I asked.

"Having the liberty to do what we want. Look at us. Both in our twenties, and we still get to experience the joy of playing in the rain like when we were kids. That's what fun in adulthood is about—reminding our inner child that we can still be playful. Like this!" he said.

There was a big puddle of water in front of us. He scooped up some water and looked me straight in the eyes.

"Ben, don't you dare! I swear if you throw that water at me, I'm out of here. We are never going camping again," I said, very seriously.

He threw the water, splashing my torso. My jaw dropped.

"Ben! Are you serious? Look at my shirt!" I said, noticing a few droplets of dirt on it.

He was laughing his head off.

"You're lucky I'm in a wheelchair. You'd be running by now," I said, laughing.

"I'm sorry. I didn't know the water was so dirty. My bad," he said, still laughing.

"And then you called the cute squirrel a rat," I said.

"Ah, I'm offended. Should I run into the woods?" he said.

We both laughed.

We walked for a few more minutes until we finally made it back to our campsite. The rain had stopped, and Ben grabbed our backpacks with clothes and towels from the car. He handed me my towel as he took off his shirt. I couldn't help but stare at his lean physique while trying not to be weird about it. I dried myself as much as I could.

"Are we going to the bathrooms so I can change?" I asked.

"Yeah, let's go. Do you need help?" he asked.

"I need you to pass me my clothes while I change," I said.

"No problem," he said.

When we arrived at the bathrooms, there was no unisex family bathroom, so we decided to enter the women's bathroom. Luckily, it had an accessible stall.

"Do you want me to wait for you out here?" he asked.

"No, come inside the stall with me so you can help me," I said.

"Okay, let me know how to help," he said.

"Hand me my towel. I'm going to take all my wet clothes off," I said.

He handed me my towel and turned around.

"Can you pass me my underwear and bra? They're at the bottom of the backpack," I said.

"The light blue ones?" he asked.

"Yes, those ones and the white bra," I said.

He passed me my underwear like someone passing a note under a desk in school without looking. I put them on, struggling a bit with my bottoms.

"I got them on. Now pass me my jean shorts," I said.

"There you go," he said.

"And my navy blue tank top," I said.

"Here!" he said.

I put them on.

"I'm done. You can turn around now," I said.

"I'm not going to lie, I wanted to peek so bad," he said.

"Well, you had your chance. I'm joking," I said.

"I'm so hungry," Benson said.

"We have pre-made chicken wraps from the supermarket. We can eat that. Are we going to make the s'mores?" I asked as we went back to our campsite.

"Oh, absolutely. That's going to be the highlight of our trip," he said.

We sat down at the picnic table and enjoyed our subs. It had cooled down a bit.

"I forgot to bring a jacket," I said.

"I brought a flannel. It's in the car. Let me get it for you," Ben said.

"Here you go," he said as he handed me his dark green flannel.

I put it on, and it had a nice smell of men's cologne that made me snuggle up like a cozy blanket.

"Thank you! I'm going to keep it since you ruined my shirt earlier," I said sarcastically.

He laughed.

"Hey! I already apologized for that. You can keep it if it reminds you of me," he said.

"Washing the stains will," I smiled.

It was getting dark. We started a fire using a match kit specifically for campfires. The warm glow of the fire illuminated our faces as the night got darker. We took some sticks from the ground to use as skewers since we forgot to buy roasting sticks. Benson sat next to me, and we held our improvised skewers over the fire.

"How do you know when the marshmallow is done?" I asked.

"When it starts getting golden brown," he said.

"I think mine is a little overdone," I said, looking at the black spots on the marshmallow.

"Let me get you a new one. Yours is completely black," he said, poking a new marshmallow onto the stick.

I started over, making sure not to burn it this time.

"Did I tell you I started taking a painting workshop this past week?" I asked, rotating my stick over the fire.

"No. How did it go?" he asked curiously.

"It went great. For our first assignment we painted a canvas to represent how we've been feeling lately. This is what I painted," I said, showing him a photo of my painting on my phone.

"Nice! You're really good at it. What's the feeling you're trying to portray?" he asked.

"It's supposed to show how we can find beauty in pain. That's why I painted both living and dead flowers," I said.

"I can see that. You're so creative and talented. I can totally see you one day exhibiting your paintings in an art gallery," he said.

"Who knows? Maybe I'll be the next Van Gogh," I said, smiling.

"What about you? What are you passionate about? I remember you said you wanted to study psychology. Is that something you see yourself doing in the future?" I asked.

"Oh, absolutely. Since I was a kid, I've always had this empathy towards others. It's so interesting to me that we can guide our thoughts to hopefully live happier lives. That's how I want to contribute to the world," he said.

"That's beautiful, Ben. I know if that's your plan, everything will align for you to achieve whatever your heart desires," I said.

"Thank you! I really appreciate that," he said.

"This is probably one of the best things I've ever eaten," I said, as we both took a second bite of our freshly melted s'mores.

"I could easily eat like three of them," Ben said.

"They are so good," I said.

As I looked around, I saw the beautiful dark blue and purple sky full of stars. A sky speckled with tiny but bright stars that made it shine from within. It was breathtaking. You could also see the black silhouette of each tree in the distance, making the view look like a perfect landscape painting. The crackling noise of the campfire and the sound of the crickets created the perfect symphony, grounding us in nature.

"Wow! Earth never stops impressing me. Look at the stars!" I said.

"I know. They're beautiful, just like you!" he said.

I smiled and blushed at the same time.

"Why are you laughing? It's true. I think you're the sweetest, most down-to-earth, and beautiful woman I've ever met," he said.

"Do you think so?" I asked.

"Yeah! And I like you a lot," he said.

Something about those words left me speechless. We are always searching for people who see us for who we truly are, and here I had someone expressing their feelings to me, and I didn't even know what to say.

"I like you a lot too. I think you're an incredible human being. I love how you see the world and how you stay positive even when life hasn't gone the way you wanted it to. You are beautiful not only on the outside but for who you are on the inside. I think you're one of a kind," I said, relieved to finally express my feelings.

He leaned in for a kiss, and I followed. Butterflies formed in my stomach, and serotonin rushed through my veins. At that moment, everything went silent. My love for him grew as I got closer. I cared for him so deeply that it reflected in that kiss. I gave him a hug, my head resting on his shoulder. Everything felt right.

The night came to an end. We got inside the tent, and he put my wheelchair in the car. We talked for another hour or so before cuddling in our sleeping bags. My head rested on his chest, his arm around me. The calm of the night enveloped us like the softest silk blanket. This was probably one of the best days of my life.

# Chapter 12
## Questions at the Dinner Table

We came back from our camping trip around 4:35 p.m. As we pulled into my parents' driveway, we saw my mom tending to her flowers. It was Sunday, the day she usually did projects around the house. She wore a chin-strap straw gardening hat and her signature light pink rose gloves.

"Hi, Mom!" I said from the car window.

"Hi, sweetie. You're finally home," she said.

"Mom, come meet Benson!" I said.

She took off her gardening gloves and rinsed her hands with the garden hose.

"Hi, Benson! It's so nice to finally meet you. I'm Heather," she said.

"Nice to meet you too," he said.

"How was the trip?" Mom asked.

"We had so much fun. Who knew that I would enjoy nature so much?" I said.

"I think her favorite part was the s'mores we ate," Ben said.

"They were really good," I said, nodding. "But, Mom, stargazing at night was unbelievably gorgeous."

"That's wonderful. I told you nature does wonders for the mind. I'm glad you both enjoyed your trip," she said.

"Benson, are you from around here?" Mom asked.

"The apartment complex where I live is about twenty to thirty minutes from here," he said.

"Oh wow, that's relatively close," she said.

"Yeah, it's not that far," he said.

"Do you want to join us for dinner? I always make extra food," Mom said.

"What's for dinner?" I asked.

"I'm making barbecue chicken, corn on the cob, and mashed potatoes. We would be more than happy if you joined us," she said.

"Sure! I would love to," Ben said.

"Would you like something to drink?" Mom asked.

"No, I'm good, thank you," he said.

"I drank almost half my water bottle on the way here, but thank you for asking," I said.

"I'm going to finish making dinner. If you need anything, let me know," she said.

Ben got my wheelchair from the car so I could transfer to it. We took out the food we didn't end up using, and I went inside to set it on the kitchen counter. Then we sat on the porch.

"This neighborhood is so quiet," Ben said.

"I know. Sometimes I think it's extremely lonely. Nothing like when I was little and kids used to play outside all the time. I guess tablets are the new source of entertainment for kids nowadays, but I appreciate the peace and quiet," I said, looking at the street. "Come inside, let me introduce you to my father."

"Dad! I want you to meet someone," I yelled from the living room.

"I'm in the backyard," Dad shouted.

Dad was fixing our wooden fence. He had all his woodworking tools on a plastic foldable table that he always stored in the garage.

"Dad, this is Benson!" I said.

"Hey! How's it going? I'm James," Dad said, extending his hand to greet him.

"Nice to meet you, sir," Ben said, shaking his hand.

"You can call me James. What are you guys up to?" Dad asked.

"We arrived from our camping trip about fifteen minutes ago. Dad, you would have loved it. The view of the woods and everything was something you would have really enjoyed," I said.

"Did you build a campfire and everything?" Dad asked.

"We did. We used these fire starters that you just light at one end, and they immediately start a fire," Ben said.

"So you're telling me you didn't start it with rocks and sticks?" Dad said, smiling.

"We're in the twenty-first century, not the eighteen hundreds, Dad," I said.

"That would be an interesting challenge," Dad said.

"Spending four hours to start a fire?" I said.

"That's the whole point of being out in nature," Dad said.

"The cedar wood looks good on the fence," Ben said, staring at Dad's progress.

"Thank you. I have to secure it with a few more screws, and my job is done for the day," Dad said.

"I used to help my dad build fences when I was growing up. I can recognize cedar and pine wood from a distance," Ben said.

I watched as Dad and Ben talked for twenty minutes about power tools and building supplies they had used. It amazed me how much I still didn't know about Ben. It was comforting watching them bond over construction supplies. It was like watching a father and son interact. Knowing that Ben didn't have a great relationship with his parents broke my heart. Who wouldn't appreciate the genuinely good person he is? He has been selfless, caring, and loving since the day we met.

"Madison, dinner is ready," Mom said from the back door.

We all sat at the dining table, where there were three platters of food at the center. We each had a plate, silver cutlery, and a water bottle. As we began to serve ourselves some delicious homemade food, my mom decided to break the ice.

"Benson, what do you do for a living?" Mom asked.

"I'm a bartender at a sports bar/restaurant called the Game Time Grill. I've been working there for the past three years," Ben said.

"Do you plan to work there all your life?" Dad asked.

"Dad!" I said, surprised by how rude that sounded.

"Sorry, I didn't mean it like that," Dad said.

"Don't worry about it. Actually, I have been applying to different colleges to start my bachelor's degree in psychology," Ben said.

"That's wonderful. The need for mental health services is on the rise. With all these technological advances, everyone is living in this digital bubble, and human connection is getting lost. People are lonelier than ever. That's very nice," Mom said.

"Thank you! Hopefully, one day, I'll have my own practice," Ben said.

"Can you believe Madison dropped out this semester from her accounting degree? She only had one year left to graduate," Dad said.

"Yeah, she told me. I think she made the right decision for herself. Doing something you don't like for a career can make you very unhappy. Life is too short to not do what we love," Ben said.

"She has years ahead of her to figure it out," Mom said, sipping her water.

"And what are your intentions with my daughter?" Dad asked, staring directly at Ben.

At that point, I thought inviting Benson for dinner was a bad idea. The whole questioning felt like a job interview with my parents. I knew Dad was protective, but I felt embarrassed.

"I like her a lot. I would love to pursue a relationship with her. We're getting to know each other, and from what I've experienced, she is truly a wonderful person," Ben said.

Mom looked at me like she was the one who had fallen in love.

"And what do you think about her being in a wheelchair? For us, there is nothing wrong with that, but I want to ensure that people have the right intentions and respect for her as we do. Living with a disability can be challenging, and from a relationship perspective, I just want to know that she will be okay and that you're okay with that," Dad said.

"I completely understand. I don't see her any differently whether she's walking or using a wheelchair. Madison is a great person, and that's what caught my attention about her from the day we met. I have a lot of respect for her and I'm willing to be by her side for whatever she needs," Ben said.

"I appreciate that. I'm just looking out for her. You seem like a very smart and nice guy," Dad said.

"No, I get where you're coming from, and thank you for the compliment," Ben said.

Silence surrounded the table, broken only by the sound of cutlery clashing with the ceramic plates. It got awkward after my dad decided to truly express his feelings.

"Mrs. Heather, the grilled chicken is so good," Ben said.

"Thank you, there's more if you want," Mom said. "It's probably the barbecue sauce," she added.

"No, I'm good. I think I'm already getting full," Ben said.

"Well, I think you two make a cute couple. Treat each other with respect and honesty. That's the key to a good relationship. I have no doubts that your relationship will develop into something beautiful," Mom said out of nowhere. "Maddic, you've been silent this entire time. What are you thinking?" she asked.

"I'm just processing this whole conversation. Being twenty-two and still being overprotected is something that caught me off guard, to be honest," I said.

"We are just looking out for you, that's all!" Dad said.

"That's fine! You don't have to worry about me. I know how to look out for myself," I said.

Everything about that conversation was upsetting. I felt like I was being treated like a teenager. It was so upsetting that I went from living on my own to living with my parents again. I was embarrassed that the conversation centered around whether someone would be okay with me being in a wheelchair.

The situation reminded me why I crave independence. Feeling less worthy just because my body is different from others is something I did not expect to experience in my adulthood. Everything hit me harder than it should have. I guess my frustration was building inside me. I'm trying hard every day to stay afloat, and it seems like nothing goes my way these days.

I took my plate to the kitchen and went outside. I took a deep breath and just stared at the sky in the distance. I heard the front door close behind me.

"Hey! Are you okay?" Ben said.

"Yeah! I'm feeling better. I just needed some fresh air," I said, still upset.

"Talk to me. Why are you upset?" Ben said, sitting on the floor next to me.

"I just feel like I'm not good enough, that's all," I said, tucking my hair behind my ear.

"And why do you think that?" he asked.

"Because this is not how I pictured my life at twenty-two," I said.

"And how did you picture it?" he asked.

"Definitely not like this. I always had a plan for everything. Now everything feels like I've gone a thousand steps back," I said, trying to coherently express my thoughts.

"Don't see it like that! Everyone's journey is different. Life has a different path for you, and maybe you can't see it right now, but one day you will look back and realize that you were at the right place at the right time. I believe we all have a purpose in life. You are still here. That's all that matters. Everything is going to be okay," he said.

"Oh my god, you should really be a psychologist," I said, smiling.

He smiled. "I should."

"You are going to be great at it," I said, staring into his eyes.

"Can I give you a hug?" he asked.

I nodded.

"I'm so glad we crossed paths," he whispered while we hugged.

Those words lifted every dark feeling and blurred thought that inhabited my mind.

"I love you," I said without hesitation.

"I love you too," he said.

When we went back inside, we offered to do the dishes and clean up the dining room table. I grabbed plate by plate and stacked them on my lap. Ben took the dishes from my lap and washed them by hand at the sink. After half an hour of cleaning, I decided to show Ben the rest of the house where I grew up. As I was showing him my room, the first thing he noticed was my record player.

"You weren't lying when you said you loved music. Look at all these records," he said, skimming through the vinyls with his hands.

"There was a period in my life where I used to go to a local vinyl store once a month to buy a new record to add to my collection. I was obsessed with them," I said.

"Why did you stop collecting them?" he asked.

"I was running out of space. If it were up to me, my room would be filled with vinyls all over the place," I said.

He sat on my bed and took a quick glance around my room.

"You even have a disco ball? What? You have a full club in your bedroom," he said.

"Pretty much. Before my accident, music was a big part of my life. I used to go to every concert or music festival that I could. I used to work in my college library and put money aside just for my music-related outings," I said.

"What about now?" he asked.

"Well, I'm not working, so there's that," I said.

"There are a lot of places with live music where you don't have to spend a lot of money to have a good time. Now I have more ideas on where we should go next time we go out," he said.

"We still need to go to a concert together," I said.

"We have to. I truly love your room. It's a reflection of who you are," he said as he got up from the bed. "I better get going. It's getting late, and I have to work an early shift tomorrow. I want to say goodbye to your parents before I leave."

I nodded. We walked down the hallway where my parents were sitting on the couch watching a show on TV.

"Thank you for inviting me over for dinner. I had a great time getting to know you both. I'm going to head out; I have an early shift tomorrow," Ben said.

"It was a pleasure meeting you, Benson. Remember, this is your home whenever you are around. You are part of the family now," Mom said.

"Thank you! The food was delightful," he said, giving Mom a kiss on the cheek.

"James, it was a pleasure," he said, shaking Dad's hand.

"Pleasure was mine. Next time, if I need help with building something, I'm going to call you," Dad said with a sarcastic tone.

"Please do. I'll bring my power tools," Ben said with a smile.

"Well, I better get going," Ben said.

"Bye, Ben!" Mom said.

"Drive safe," Dad said.

It was completely dark now. We headed down the concrete pathway to the driveway where his car was parked.

"I had a great time with you these past two days," Ben said.

"Me too," I said.

"And I think you have the nicest parents I've ever met. They care about you a lot," he said.

"I know. Sometimes I take them for granted," I said.

"Don't be so hard on yourself or them. You're doing great. You've got each other," he said as he took his key out of his pocket.

"Before you go, I wanted to tell you that this weekend was one of the best experiences of my life. You pushed me out of my shell and I had an amazing time with you. I appreciate you more than you know. You genuinely make me so happy," I said.

"Does this mean that you're officially my girlfriend?" he asked.

"Well, I don't kiss strangers on the mouth just because, or much less cuddle with them in a tent. It's not my thing," I said.

He laughed.

"I love everything about you," he said, looking straight into my eyes, leaning on the passenger door of his car.

His words touched my soul. Every time he expressed his love for me, a rush of peacefulness took over my body. His words meant everything to me.

"I love everything about you too," I said.

We kissed, and I hugged him goodbye.

# Chapter 13
## Discovering My Potential

Arriving at my second art workshop was exciting. I instantly noticed that half of the class didn't show up. We went from thirteen people to about nine for our second session. To me, it was fine; the fewer people, the more one-on-one time we could have with our instructor to improve our techniques. I sat at the same table as the first time, and Emily decided to do the same.

Emily is the true definition of someone who loves to express their creative side. This is the second time I have seen her wearing this wavy line art as eye shadow in a neon shade of green. She has a short bob haircut with platinum blonde lowlights that give depth to her light brown hair. Her side-parted hair, combined with her colorful wardrobe, makes her look very fun to be around.

"Hi Emily! How are you?" I asked.

"Good, how are you?" she said.

"I'm doing great. Excited for today's session."

"Last week I didn't say anything, but I loved your bouquet of daisies painting," she said.

"Thank you! I'm excited to see what we get to create today."

"I know, right?" she said.

Alex came through the door and ordered us to take a seat. He took a quick look at each of us as if he was counting for attendance.

"I already see that the class has reduced a little bit. That's alright. It's completely normal and expected. I just want to say thank you for being here. I know I have said it a thousand times, but it means a lot to me that you want to be here. Today we are going to quickly hop on our project for the day. I want you to choose someone to pair with for today's session, as we are going to work as a team. If someone doesn't end up in a pair, please join another team to make a group of three since we have an odd number today."

"Emily, do you want to be my teammate?" I asked.

"I would love to," she responded.

"Now that you've all paired up, our theme for this week is texture," Alex said.

"Ahhh," a classmate exhaled.

"I heard someone saying 'ahhh' in the back. It's going to be fun, I promise. We usually see artwork in a two-dimensional form, but today we're going full 3D." Alex said as he put on some old movie theater 3D glasses.

The entire room laughed. It was so unexpected of him.

"They look fire on you!" a guy said.

"I knew one day they'd come in handy. Anyway, as I was saying, sometimes we can make our artwork stand out by providing texture. Texture adds a sense of physicality to an artwork by creating an illusion of three-dimensional surfaces and shapes that can be seen and felt. This physicality helps make the artwork more realistic, immersive, and engaging. So for today's assignment, I have different materials that you can use to create a piece of art on your canvases, with the goal of portraying the importance of texture in art," he said. "Be creative, and the time starts now. I don't know why I said that. This is not a reality TV competition. Remember to have fun. You can go now and get your materials."

Emily and I went to the back of the studio. There were two tables in the middle with all sorts of different materials: fabrics in a variety of colors, jewelry-making beads, stickers, crafting paper, scissors, glues, and all sorts of crafting materials you can imagine.

"What are you thinking?" I asked Emily.

"Maybe we can grab some foam and create abstract art with different layers," she said.

"We can stack them to create different height levels like stairs," I said.

"Oh my god, yes! Let's do that," she said excitedly.

We grabbed foam, a hot glue gun, and a precision knife from the table. With our materials in hand, we agreed to cut wavy shapes to create curves to contrast the rectangular shape of the canvas.

"Have you always been into art?" I asked while focusing on cutting the foam.

"Since I was a little girl. I have always worked in the corporate world, but now that I'm thirty-two, I have realized that life is too short not to do what we love. So I'm exploring different art forms for fun, hoping to one day open my own business that fulfills my creative needs. What about you?" she said.

"I have a similar path, but I haven't navigated the corporate world. I'm the same: I have a passion for anything creative, and I want to go for it and maybe make a living from it. That would be my dream," I said.

"I totally get it. I think the exact same way. Are you okay with the idea of me making a circle to put somewhere with our shapes?" she asked, holding a piece of foam board.

"Of course. Go ahead. You don't have to ask. I'm okay with whatever idea you come up with. Art shouldn't be that serious," I said.

"Don't tell that to a perfectionist. I'll overthink it for days," Emily said.

We took the hot glue and started attaching the foam to the canvas. It was like creating a puzzle. Each piece overlapped, creating an interesting, layered piece.

"Totally random question..." Emily began.

Here we go again, I thought. Should I start creating false scenarios to escape reliving the traumatic accident that still haunts me every day?

"It was a car accident," I said before she could finish.

"What?" she said, confused.

"I just wanted to ask if you're good with the idea of painting the whole canvas the same color. I'm thinking of a dark olive green," she said.

"Yeah, let's go with that. I actually love that shade of green," I said, overthinking how stupid I had sounded a few seconds ago.

For a few minutes, I didn't know what to say. My social battery was running low, so I concentrated on painting the canvas with our selected green shade. Every time I get social anxiety, I come up with the most random questions to keep the conversation going.

"How are you thirty-two? You look so young. I thought you were in your twenties," I said.

"I get that a lot, but I'm actually a millennial. Let me guess your age! Twenty-five?" she said.

"Close. Lower," I said.

"Twenty-one?" she guessed.

"Twenty-two. I'm exactly a decade younger than you," I said.

"You saying it like that makes me feel really old," she said.

"Does life get easier in your thirties?" I asked.

"I don't think so. That's a really good question," she said while helping me paint the foam. "I would say you care less about the opinion of others, but the feeling of being lost and not knowing what I'm doing with my life never goes away. I think you keep faking it until you make it for the rest of your life. That's how life is. I like to think that's how we all go through it. Trust the universe; life will lead you exactly where you need to go," she said while looking at our creation from the side of the table.

"So it's not that bad," I said.

"Not at all. You need to stay optimistic even when you go through those unavoidable hardships. At the end of the day, everything works out just fine or better than you imagined," she said.

"That's a great way to see life. Look at us! Getting inspired by just doing some arts and crafts," I said, smiling.

"I know. I don't know how our conversation turned into a deep existential topic just from painting a canvas," she said.

"I guess you can find meaning in anything," I said.

We ended our project, and we were proud of it. As in our previous workshop, Alex had all of us explain our work to the rest of the group. That evening, I felt so inspired. I don't know if it was my conversation with Emily that made something click in my head, but art is something I want to fully invest my time in. For the first time in my life, I felt like this was something I truly enjoyed doing.

While we were cleaning up our table, I exchanged phone numbers with Emily. We had so much in common that our interactions always flowed with ease. Everyone said goodbye, and I waited for my mom to pick me up next to a concrete pillar facing the parking lot outside the studio.

As I was scrolling on my phone, I heard Alex closing up the studio behind me.

"Madison, do you need a ride?" Alex asked.

"No. I'm just waiting for my mother to finish grabbing some groceries real quick before she picks me up, but thank you for asking," I said.

"No problem," he said.

I kept scrolling through some random news articles on my phone to kill time when I heard someone approaching me.

"Do you mind if I keep you company while your mother picks you up? The parking lot is completely empty. I don't want to leave you alone, especially since there are so many random people around here all the time," Alex said.

"Not at all," I said.

He sat on the floor next to me.

"Wow, look at that sunset," he said.

As I looked up, he was right. Vibrant glowing orange tones intertwined with pale hues of gray clouds painted the whole sky.

"That's a real-life painting," I said.

"And sometimes we forget that it's there for us to appreciate," he said. "By the way, I have been very impressed with your past two projects. I see something there. You are naturally very talented."

"You think?" I said, surprised.

"I think you have an undiscovered talent. I can't imagine how good you can get with more practice. With a few more techniques, I think you have something to work on. Who knows? Maybe one day you could be showcasing your work in an art gallery," he said.

"Really? To be honest, I don't think I'm on that level yet," I said.

"But you could be. I see your potential," he said.

"Thank you!" I said.

"You're more than welcome. If you ever need anything from me to help with your work or to teach you something, please don't hesitate to let me know. That's why I'm here," he said.

"I will. I promise," I said.

Looking through the parking lot, I saw my mom approaching.

"My mom is here," I said.

"Do you need help getting in the car?" Alex asked.

"No. I can transfer myself from my chair, but thank you," I said.

"Let me at least help you load the wheelchair into the car," he said, getting up from the floor.

I truly didn't need his help, but I couldn't turn down his kind offer. He walked by my side all the way to where my mother had parked in the handicap spot. My mom rolled down the car window.

"Sorry I was late. There was a line at the supermarket," Mom said.

We walked to the passenger side of the car as my mom opened the door from the inside.

"Hi! I'm Alex, Madison's art instructor," he said.

"Nice to meet you, Alex! I'm Heather, Madison's mom. I'm so sorry that I kept you waiting," she said.

"That's okay, Mom. Don't worry about it," I said.

I transferred from my chair to the passenger seat while I told Alex how to remove the wheels from the wheelchair. He picked it up and carefully put it in the back seat.

"All set. It's lighter than I thought," he said.

"It is. The titanium frame is lighter than other materials," I said.

"I don't know why I thought it was going to be as heavy as a bicycle," he said.

"Not even close. Thank you for your help. I appreciate it," I said.

"No problem. It was nice meeting you, Heather. Madison, see you next week," Alex said.

"Nice meeting you too," Mom said.

"Bye!" Mom and I said at the same time.

"Bye!" he said.

"He seems like such a lovely young man," Mom said.

"He's really sweet," I said.

"Lately, you have been meeting these great, handsome men. That was not my case back in the day," she said.

"Mom, he's just my art instructor," I said, trying to figure out what she really meant.

"Don't look at me like that. I was just saying that lately, you are meeting good people," she said.

"We don't know him. And besides, I'm dating Ben. Let's go home before you start confusing me with your real-life romance book tropes," I said in a playful tone.

# Chapter 14
## Finding Myself Again

I've spent the last couple of days gathering painting supplies with my parents so I can have a corner in my room to paint, without waiting for my weekly workshop. We found an old plastic foldable table in the garage, usually reserved for holiday gatherings, and set it up right in front of my bedroom window. We rearranged the room, making sure the table faced the window so I could draw inspiration from the outside world instead of staring at a blank wall. My dad bought me two medium-sized canvases, some oil paints, and a set of brushes. As I was taking the brushes out of their plastic packaging and placing them in a glass jar, my phone rang.

"Hello," I said.

"Hi, babe. What are you up to?" Ben asked?.

"I'm finishing up setting a corner in my bedroom so I can have a space where I can paint," I said.

"Oh nice! Where did you end up putting it?" he asked.

"Right in front of the window," I said, staring at the backyard.

"Makes sense. It's better than staring at a wall, especially your cold white walls," he said.

"Hey, white is aesthetically pleasing, and you can change the color of your decor whenever you like without having to change the color of your walls," I said.

"White walls can be boring," he said.

"Ben. I'm going to act like you didn't say anything. Speaking of walls, when are you going to take me to see your apartment? I want to see where you live. I could guess that you live on an upper floor," I said.

"I actually live on the first floor," he said.

"And why haven't you invited me over?" I asked.

"I don't know. I didn't know that was something you were interested in," he responded.

"Well, now I am. To be fair, I didn't know you that well," I said.

"Taking women back to my place is not something I do often," he said.

"But you used to? How much?" I asked.

"Pretty frequently. I blame it on working as a bartender," he said.

"And that justifies you sleeping with a lot of girls?" I said.

"No. It sounds like it's bothering you a little," he said.

"No. I'm just curious. So you slept with them just for fun?" I asked.

"Looking back at it now, I guess so," he said.

"And what did you get out of that?" I asked.

"Are we really doing this right now? This is hilarious. Nothing. I got nothing out of it. Just a temporary pleasure that led to nowhere. That's why I stopped doing it," he said.

"Interesting," I said.

"Are you mad?" he asked.

"No. Why would I be mad? We are not perfect in any way. Who am I to judge?" I said.

"Do you have any love stories you want to share?" he asked.

"I haven't dated a lot, to be completely honest. I only had a high school boyfriend. That's it," I said.

"What? How?" he asked.

"I love your surprised reaction. Yeah. I don't think I'm the kind of person who puts all their energy into looking for a partner. I tend to focus on the things I want to accomplish for my personal growth. I've always been like that. I don't need somebody," I said.

"You don't have to stop your life just because you are with someone. You can have someone who supports you and cheers you on in whatever you're pursuing," he said.

"You've got a valid point," I said.

"That's what I like about you. You are different from any girl that I have met before. Now I have a different kind of love for you," he said.

"Because I have a disability?" I asked.

"No. I told you that does not even cross my mind. You are who you are, and I see it. I see you for who you are. I care about you a lot. That's the kind of love that I was looking for. I didn't know what I wanted, but now it is really clear to me. I was looking for someone that I care deeply for," he said.

"You're always saying the sweetest things, and I usually don't know how to respond," I said.

"That's okay. You don't always have to say something back," he said.

"It really does mean a lot that you see me like that, and I care about you a lot too. You are the best thing that happened to me these past few weeks," I said.

"Let's hug it out through the phone," he said.

"What? What do you mean?" I asked, laughing. "I'm not mad at you,"

"That would be so funny," he said.

"You are silly," I said.

"So, I'll pick you up this Thursday so we can have dinner at my place?" he asked.

"Are you going to cook for me?" I asked.

"I'm pretty decent at making a good lasagna. Do you like lasagna?" he asked.

"I love lasagna, especially with garlic bread. I'm getting hungry right now just thinking about it," I said.

"Uff, bring a bottle of mouthwash then," he said.

"Are you saying we are not going to have garlic smooches?" I asked.

"Nope. Six feet apart from each other," he said.

"We can just add a tiny amount of garlic. Now that I think about it, you know what could be a great idea?" I said.

"What?" he asked.

"We should cook together so we can both share our ways of preparing a meal. That way we can learn from each other," I said.

"That sounds like a great idea," he said.

"It sure does. Quality time, I would say," I said.

"It sure is," he said.

A moment of silence came between our phone conversation.

"I'm going to let you go so you can work on your canvas," he said.

"Yeah. I should start doing that," I said as I looked at my brand new oil paints.

"I'm going to let you go now. Talk to you later," he said. "Love you."

"Love you too. Bye!" I said.

"Bye," he said.

The sun is warm on my shoulders as I sit in my room, the canvas before me still a blank promise. I dip my brush into a vibrant blue, watching the color drip lazily before pressing it to the canvas. The first stroke is always the hardest, but once it's there, the rest follows like a river finding its path. As the blues and greens begin to take shape, I find my mind drifting, lost in the fluid motions of painting.

I wasn't always like this. The brush, the canvas, these were strangers to me once. Before the accident, my life was a whirlwind of activity, never slowing down, never stopping to breathe. I was always in motion, always running toward the next goal, the next achievement. It's strange how everything changed in an instant, how a single moment could redefine everything I thought I knew about myself.

When the doctors told me I would never walk again, it felt like the ground had been ripped from beneath my feet. I was plunged into a world of stillness, forced to confront a new reality where my legs were lifeless, and my dreams seemed just as paralyzed. The days that followed were a blur of anger, grief, and despair. But somewhere amidst the chaos, I found myself again.

As I blend the colors on my palette, I realize how much I've changed. Painting has taught me patience, something I sorely lacked before. Each stroke, each careful application of color, is a meditation, a way to connect with the world in a manner I never knew possible. It's funny, in a way, how losing the use of my legs has given me a new perspective on life, a new way to move forward.

I look at the canvas, now alive with swirls of blue and green, a representation of the garden in front of me. Nature continues to thrive, indifferent to my struggles, yet offering solace in its beauty. The flowers bloom, the trees sway, and the sky remains vast and endless. And here I am, a part of it all, even in this new form.

My life isn't what I planned, but maybe that's okay. The accident took away my ability to walk, but it gave me something in return, a chance to rediscover myself, to find strength in vulnerability, and to appreciate the world from a different vantage point. Every day is a new canvas, a new opportunity to create something beautiful, despite the challenges.

As I add the final touches to my painting, I feel a sense of calm wash over me. I may be a paraplegic, but I am not paralyzed. I am still moving forward, still creating, still living. And at this moment, that's more than enough.

Dad came into the room.

"Wow, Maddie! That's a beautiful painting. It looks exactly like our backyard," he said.

"Look, I even painted your unfinished fence," I said.

"Every detail is exactly as it is in real life," he said, studying the painting.

"I still have to finish the sky, but I think that's enough for today," I said.

"You're doing a great job, and you have the talent for it. If this is something you want to pursue in life, go for it!" he said.

"You're not mad that I dropped out of college?" I asked.

"Why would I be mad? I just want the best for you. I want you to do what makes you happy. I don't want you to feel pressured to do something you don't enjoy. That's a miserable way to live," he said.

"Thanks, Dad! I promise you I'm going to give it my all," I said.

"You don't need to promise me anything. Everything you do, do it for you. At the end of the day, what you do with your life is for you, nobody else," he said.

I nodded.

"Next time, I want a portrait of me," he said.

"For what?" I asked.

"To look at myself every day and remind myself of how great I am," he said.

"Oh god, that's a very narcissistic thing to say. Where do you want to hang it up? Next to our entryway door?" I asked, smiling.

He laughed.

"That's a horrible idea. Your mom would kill me," he said. "But seriously, I'm proud of you. You've handled everything so well. I love you."

"I love you too, Dad," I said.

"If you need anything, let me know," he said.

"I'm kind of hungry. I could use a personal chef right now. Any chance you're up for that?" I asked jokingly.

"I'm going to give those last touches to that fence now that you pointed that out," he said as he immediately walked away.

# Chapter 15
## Bubble of Affection

"Are you ready?" Benson asked as we stood at the front door of his apartment.

"You're making me nervous," I said.

Ben pulled the keys from his pocket and opened the door. I was speechless. He had the cutest one-bedroom apartment, with gray-toned hardwood floors that complemented the light gray walls. As soon as you entered the front door, the kitchen was on the right. White shaker-style cabinets and stainless steel appliances made the kitchen look modern and sleek.

"You even have a pedestal dining room table? Didn't you tell me you were struggling financially?" I asked in complete shock.

"I am. I'm still living paycheck to paycheck," he said, smiling.

Looking at the living room, everything was neatly organized. A light brown leather couch centered against the living room wall separated his bedroom from his living space. Two accent chairs with an accent table faced the entryway view, and behind them, a window illuminated the whole space with natural light.

"You have a beautiful one-bedroom apartment," I said, looking around.

"Thank you! I tried my best to decorate it the way I wanted to," he said, looking at the living room.

As I peeked into the living room, I couldn't help but notice a picture frame sitting on the TV stand. It looked like Ben as a kid with two adults and an older child next to him.

"Are these your parents?" I asked, holding the light oak picture frame.

"Yep, that's me and my older brother," he said, pointing with his finger.

"Your mother is so pretty. You kind of look like her," I said, staring at his mother's perfectly straight hair.

"You think?" he asked.

"You look so much like her. You are the male version of her," I said as I looked at the picture and then back at him.

"How long has it been since you last talked to her?" I asked.

"A really long time," he said.

"Ben, life is really short. We don't know what could happen tomorrow. You should give them a chance," I said.

"Ahh, I don't know about that," Ben said.

"The older I get, the more I understand that no one has a clue what they are doing in life. Maybe they didn't understand how to love someone. We all have a different idea of love. Maybe they loved you in a different way. Maybe forgiving people is the best thing we can do to heal ourselves," I said as I moved closer to give him a hug.

"I love you," he said as he rested his head on my shoulder.

"I love you too," I said.

"Look what I got for dinner!" he said, holding a bottle of red wine from the kitchen counter.

"We're going to have the full Italian restaurant experience," I said.

"Pretty much. Better than Olive Garden for sure," he said.

"I hope so," I said.

"Would you like to help me start cooking the ground beef?" Ben asked.

"Let me wash my hands first," I replied.

Ben took out the ground beef, plopped it into a skillet, and broke it down with a wooden spatula.

"Do you mind if we listen to some music?" he said.

"No, not at all. A restaurant and a concert at the same time," I said.

Billie Eilish's "The Greatest" came on from a small speaker in the kitchen corner.

"Have you heard it before?" he asked.

"Once, but I haven't fully heard her new album," I said.

"What? It's so good," he said.

He took the spatula and started using it as a microphone. The song began with a slow melody but then had an intense drop.

"Man, I'm the greatest!" he suddenly sang out loud.

I immediately started laughing. He was so unserious. I had never seen him like this. He's opening up to me more each day. I love him more and more as time goes on. I have never felt this kind of love for someone in my life before. He makes my life better. I hope he truly believes that he is the greatest because that's exactly how I see him.

We continued making the lasagna at the dining room table. I helped with layering the pasta while Ben loaded the meat and cheese. Something about cooking together for the first time felt like a bonding experience. I learned that Ben doesn't like cream cheese in his lasagna, while I shared that my preference for al dente pasta comes from disliking soggy textures in my food. We finished building our Italian delicacy and placed it in the oven on the broil setting to get a crispy golden cheese layer.

We decided to skip the garlic bread this time but promised each other to be ten feet away from each other for our next garlic bread date night. The lasagna came out perfectly, with no signs of burnt cheese on the sides. As we took it out of the oven, you could hear the bubbling of the cheese mixed with the tomato sauce. Ben grabbed two black plates from an upper kitchen cabinet while I grabbed the wine glasses he had previously set out.

Ben was kind enough to serve me a piece of lasagna as I poured the red wine into the freshly washed glasses.

"I swear I'm going to be completely honest," I said, cutting a small piece of the lasagna on my plate.

"Oh my god! It's good. Better than I imagined. It's really good!" I said, trying not to sound disingenuous.

"Let me try it," he said as he took a bite. "It needed more Italian seasoning in my opinion, but it's good," he said as he finished chewing his food.

"Good? It's more than good. I'm about to steal the leftovers if we don't end up eating the whole thing," I said.

"Tell me why I just pictured you rolling away with the whole ass casserole dish on your lap," he said, taking a sip of wine.

We both laughed.

"What? I'm being honest," I said.

"You are cute," he said.

"What else are you good at? You are a good cook, hardworking, organized, sweet, and a great person to be around. What's missing?" I asked.

"A lot. There are so many things I want to do. I want to have a successful career that I love. I want to travel the world. I told you before that I want to have a family one day. What about you? What do you want in life?" he asked.

"Well, I used to dream a lot and had the same mindset, but since I became paralyzed, everything has changed for me and how I view life," I said.

"In what sense?" he asked.

"In the sense that nothing is guaranteed, life doesn't always go as we plan. Never in a thousand years would it have crossed my mind that I would end up in a wheelchair. Now, I focus my energy on each day, one day at a time. I'm learning not to plan too far ahead and to focus on the present. The present is the only thing we have guaranteed," I said, taking a sip of wine.

He nodded.

"Having my artwork in a gallery one day would be nice," I said.

"Oh, that's going to happen pretty soon. You'll see," he said.

"How's your college applications going so far?" I asked.

"'I've been looking at and comparing some college tuition costs, and they are really expensive. It's tough to get a degree these days," he said.

"It is, but if this is something you really want to do, you should one hundred percent go for it," I said.

"Right! What can I lose? Only an average of nine thousand dollars in tuition a year. And that's only the tuition for a public university," he said.

"That's insane. Education should be free," I said.

"I know, right," he said as he stood up to take his plate to the kitchen.

"I bought a pre-made apple pie from the grocery store. Do you want some?" he asked.

"A small slice," I responded.

Benson cut into the pie, carefully placing a generous piece on my plate before serving himself. I watched him, noticing how his eyes crinkled slightly at the corners when he smiled, the way his hands moved with certain grace. These little details were becoming so familiar, yet each one felt like a new discovery. I felt a warmth spreading through me, not just from the pie, but from being here with Benson, sharing these moments.

"Oh, I have a good question. What was the first thing you noticed about me?" I said.

He looked thoughtful, his fork pausing mid-air. "Your laugh. It's so genuine, so full of life. I remember thinking I wanted to be the reason you laughed like that."

"The wine is kicking in?" I said.

"No, I don't need wine to tell you that," he said.

I blushed.

I took a sip of my wine, understanding him a little better with each story we exchanged. It felt like we were weaving a tapestry of shared experiences, each thread a new revelation, binding us closer together.

As the pie disappeared and the evening wore on, our conversation flowed effortlessly, touching on dreams, fears, and everything in between. I felt like I'd known Benson for a lifetime, even as I knew there was still so much more to discover.

I realized that these moments, simple, heartfelt, and honest, were what made our relationship special. We were learning each other's stories, one bite of apple pie at a time.

As night fell, we sat on the couch to watch a movie together. The room was dimly lit, the soft glow of the TV screen casting gentle shadows on the walls. Benson and I were nestled on the couch, a cozy blanket draped over us. The movie played on, but my attention was more on him than the plot. His arm was around my shoulders, drawing me close to his warmth.

I could feel the steady rise and fall of his chest, the rhythmic beat of his heart against my side. The familiarity of this moment, the ease of our closeness, filled me with a quiet contentment. I shifted slightly, resting my head against his shoulder, and felt his hand gently stroking my arm.

"Are you even watching?" he murmured, his voice a soft rumble in the quiet room.

"Barely," I admitted with a smile, turning my head to look up at him.

We lapsed into a companionable silence, the movie's soundtrack providing a soothing background. I felt his gaze on me, and when I looked up again, our eyes met. There was a softness there, a tenderness that made my heart skip a beat.

Slowly, almost hesitantly, he leaned in closer. I felt the warmth of his breath on my skin, the anticipation building between us. My eyes fluttered shut, and in the next moment, our lips met in a gentle, lingering kiss.

It started soft and sweet, a tentative exploration that soon deepened. His hand moved to cup my cheek, his thumb tracing a light, comforting pattern against my skin. I responded in kind, my fingers tangling in his hair, pulling him closer.

The world outside seemed to fade away, leaving just the two of us wrapped in our own little bubble of affection. Each kiss felt like a promise, each touch a testament to the growing connection between us.

He carried me to his bed. I had never seen Benson look so vulnerable. His usual confident demeanor was softened by a mix of tenderness and uncertainty. We both waited for this moment countless times, making sure we were both ready, that it felt right. And now, here we were, in the soft glow of his bedroom, every detail feeling both familiar and entirely new.

"Benson," I whispered, my voice barely audible over the sound of my own heartbeat. He looked up at me, his eyes filled with an intensity that made my breath catch. "Are you sure?" He whispered.

His hand covered mine, steady and warm. "I've never been more sure of anything." The words, simple yet profound, wrapped around my heart and squeezed gently.

We moved closer, our bodies aligning naturally as if drawn by an unseen force. His lips found mine, and the kiss was slow, exploratory. Every touch felt electric, sending shivers down my spine. It wasn't hurried or frantic; it was as if we had all the time in the world to savor each second.

Benson's hands roamed, not in a way that sought possession but in a way that was discovered, appreciated. I felt a rush of emotions—love, desire, trust—all mingling together in a heady cocktail that made my skin flush and my pulse race. When his fingers found the hem of my shirt, he paused, searching my eyes for permission.

I nodded, my breath hitching as he lifted the fabric, exposing more of me to him. His eyes followed his hands, his gaze reverent, making me feel beautiful in a way I hadn't before. I mirrored his actions, my own hands trembling slightly as I undressed him, revealing the lean lines of his body. The vulnerability in undressing was met with a comforting acceptance in his eyes.

We lay back on the bed, our limbs entangling, the cool sheets a stark contrast to the heat building between us. Every touch, every kiss, was a silent promise, a declaration of love spoken without words. Benson's touch was gentle, almost hesitant, but I could feel the passion simmering just beneath the surface.

When the moment finally came, it was a mix of sensations—pleasure, intimacy, and a deep, soul-stirring connection. We moved together, finding a rhythm that felt natural, right. His eyes never left mine, anchoring me, making me feel safe and cherished. There was a sweetness in our union, an unspoken understanding that this was more than just a physical act; it was the culmination of our love, our trust, our journey together.

Afterwards, we lay entwined, our breaths mingling as we came down from the heights we had scaled together. Benson brushed a strand of hair from my face, his touch tender. "I love you, Madison," he whispered, the words filled with a depth that took my breath away.

"I love you too, Benson," I replied, my voice soft but steady. At that moment, I knew that this was just the beginning of a new chapter in our story—a chapter filled with love, trust, and countless shared moments yet to come.

# Chapter 16
## A Little Tipsy

Finishing our third painting workshop felt like a breeze. For this assignment, we were allowed to paint any famous landmark of our choice, as long as we didn't repeat one that our peers had chosen. Being one of the first to pick, I chose the Eiffel Tower, although I was torn between the Big Ben and the Arc de Triomphe. My painting turned out better than I expected. I depicted the tower from a viewpoint in the Champ de Mars park. The tower stood out against the beautiful blue sky in the background. As we were getting ready to leave, Alex came to our table.

"Do you guys have any plans for tonight?" Alex asked.

"I have to catch up on some emails," Emily said.

"I've got a big pile of laundry to tackle, but why do you ask?" I said.

"I just wanted to invite you guys over for some drinks at Dave & Buster's. They're having a five-dollar late-night happy hour, but I guess you have plans," he said.

"Wait, that actually sounds like so much fun. It's been a long time since I've stepped into a Dave & Buster's. Emails can wait. Madison, I'm pretty sure your laundry can wait too," Emily said.

"I don't drive, so I'll have to ask my mom if she can take me," I said.

"Don't worry about it, we can all go in my car," Alex said.

"Let me text my mom to tell her not to pick me up then," I said.

"So, that's a yes?" he said.

I nodded.

"I'm actually excited. I used to go to Chuck E. Cheese all the time when I was ten or eleven, and it was my favorite thing about my childhood. And the pizza! Best thing on the planet," Emily said.

"Dave & Buster's is like the adult version of it, so I'm pretty sure tonight you're going to have so much fun," I said.

"Correction. We are going to have so much fun," Emily said, clapping her hands silently.

Seeing her excited about going to an adult arcade made me excited. Her energy was contagious. I could tell she was a great friend to have around.

Alex locked up the studio while Emily made sure her car was locked and that she hadn't left anything valuable inside, just in case someone broke into it in the parking lot.

"Are we ready?" Alex asked.

"Let's fucking go!" Emily said. "Sorry, I got a little too excited."

I laughed. I had a feeling tonight was going to be one of those nights where you can't stop laughing with your friends.

"Where's your car?" Emily asked as we walked through the parking lot.

"Right there!" Alex said.

"The white Tesla?" Emily asked.

"Yup," he said.

"Oh, nice! I've never been inside a Tesla before. Does it drive like a golf cart?" Emily said jokingly.

"It kinda sounds like one. I don't know if it drives like one, though. I've never driven a golf cart before," Alex said.

"What about you, Madison? Have you ever been in a Tesla?" Emily asked.

"No, it's my first time. I'm not an Elon fan, to be honest," I said.

"Me neither. Have you seen his tweets on X?" Emily asked.

"Yes. He is so out of touch with reality," I said.

"Really?" Alex asked.

"He is obsessed with the population decline and is always preaching for people to have kids as if we're all billionaires like him," I said.

"His ego is out of this world, but who can blame him? With all that money, I think I would be saying the same stupid things he's always saying on social media," Emily said.

We got inside the car, with my wheelchair secured in the trunk. Alex backed up the car while Emily commented on how her childhood pink Jeep Power Wheels made more noise than the Tesla.

"What are you guys listening to?" Alex asked.

"Billie Eilish's new album, Hit Me Hard and Soft," Emily said.

"I heard it the other day with my boyfriend, and it's so good," I said.

"So you have a boyfriend?" Alex asked, his question coming out of nowhere.

"Yeah, I've been with him for about three months," I said.

"Get it, girl! That's so cute," Emily said.

"What about you, Alex? Are you in a relationship?" Emily asked.

"No, I'm actually single as a Pringle," he said.

"What?" Emily asked.

"Yeah, so if you know anyone interested in a creative ginger, let them know I'm available," Alex said.

"We should make a marketing campaign for it and everything," Emily said.

"What about you, Emily? Are you dating someone?" I asked.

"Nope. I'm in my focusing-on-myself era. I dated a guy for six years, and after that relationship, I'm good for a while," she said.

"That's a long time," Alex said.

"It is, and the sad part is when it's over, you have to act like it never happened. Six years! You know how many things you can do in six years? That's why I'm not looking for anyone and living my best life. The peace you get from being single is out of this world. I'm contemplating staying single forever," she said.

"You don't ever worry about being lonely?" I asked.

"You can be in a relationship and still feel lonely. Not at all. My cat gives me more companionship than a man ever could. No offense, Alex," she said.

"Hey, I totally get it. Relationships are not as easy as people say they are," Alex said.

"They can be if you find the right person," I said.

"That's the hard part, especially these days when we rely on dating apps," Alex said.

"So you already have a dating marketing campaign. Ugh, but those are the worst. It's so superficial, and people are just looking for validation or waiting for the next big thing. I'd rather meet people in person. You need to get out of there ASAP," Emily said.

"I know people who have married someone they met through the apps," I said.

"That must be like 0.3% of its users," Emily said.

"The bar on those apps is really low. People don't take it seriously. Emily is right. I should delete my account," Alex said.

"Who knows, maybe you'll find your future wife tonight at Dave & Buster's," Emily said.

As we looked for a parking spot, we noticed the parking lot was packed. Who knew an adult arcade would be so busy on a weekday?

"You know what would be great right now?" Emily said.

"What?" I asked.

"Your disabled parking permit," Emily said.

"I know. I left it in my mom's car. I usually leave it there since that's how I get around," I said.

"We can walk a little bit. We're not that far from the entrance," Alex said.

We walked through the parking lot, and as we got closer to the entrance, we saw a guy smoking in his car, which was parked in an accessible parking space without a permit.

"We should totally say something about it," Emily said.

"Why waste our energy on that?" I asked.

"Why not? Madison, you need to advocate for yourself. It's totally unfair that someone who needs that parking spot has to go through the hassle of parking far away because a jerk decided to smoke in that space out of pure laziness," Emily said.

Emily approached the driver's side of the man's car.

"Excuse me, sir. I'm just wondering why you are parked in the accessible parking space without a permit," she said.

"My bad. I was just smoking a blunt for a second," the man said in a stoner tone of voice.

"Okay, but you can have your moment of relaxation over there. Someone with mobility issues could need this spot, and you're blocking them because you decided to smoke some weed for a few minutes," Emily said.

"All right, lady. I'll move," the man said angrily.

The man backed up his car and moved out of the parking spot.

"Lady? He looks older than me, even smoking that shit," she said.

We laughed.

"I can't stand the smell of it. I don't know how people do it," I said.

"You ruined his moment of meditation," Alex said.

"Nah, he's going to be way too relaxed to care," Emily said.

Walking into a Dave & Buster's feels like stepping into an electrifying wonderland. The air is filled with the sounds of laughter, buzzing arcade machines, and the occasional cheer from a victorious gamer. Bright, colorful neon lights dominate the space, casting vibrant hues across the room and reflecting off every surface. Rows upon rows of arcade games stand ready, each one a beacon of flashing LEDs and animated screens, inviting me to play. The atmosphere was a lively blend of excitement and anticipation, where every corner promises a new adventure or challenge.

The neon lights created a kaleidoscope of colors, with blues, reds, greens, and purples dancing in rhythmic patterns. Some games have swirling light displays that draw me in like a moth to a flame, while others flash rapidly, mimicking the intensity of the gameplay. It's a sensory overload in the best possible way.

We went straight to the air hockey table where I challenged Alex to a match. It was a close game. Our score was six to four making me go against Emily as the winner of our first match. Emily destroyed our second match, without letting me score a single point. We played some pac-man but unfortunately we couldn't go as far as we wanted to because those silly ghosts are faster than what my brain can process to choose which path I should take next.

We laughed a lot. We learned that Alex is a sore loser. It was funny seeing him get so disappointed over an arcade game. He wasted almost all of his points trying to get a Sonny Angel from the claw machine. Emily and Alex stomped their hearts out to the fast going arrows of the Dance Dance Revolution arcade machine while I cheered them on from the sideline.

After playing some games for a while, we decided to get a table to grab something to eat. We ordered some tequila shots and cheered to our new friendship. The alcohol burned my throat and made me cough a little.

"Are you okay?" Emily asked.

"Yeah, I'm good. That was rough," I said, my eyes watering.

As we were talking, a tall six-foot man came to the table.

"Are you guys together?" he asked, looking directly at Alex and Emily.

I was completely taken out of the equation. I felt invisible for a second. He probably thought they were both my caregivers. He didn't even acknowledge my presence, so I just looked at him and watched it all unfold. The audacity of a man to approach a group of people just to talk to a woman is something I admire. I wish I were that brave.

"No, we are just friends," Alex said.

"Do you mind if I invite you over to the bar for some drinks and a chat?" the man asked.

"I would love to," she responded.

Her answer surprised me for some reason. I had an internal gasp. I truly thought she was embracing her single era like we talked about in the car. And just like that, she disappeared into the distance. I guess all it takes is a six-foot-ish guy to sweep Emily off her feet.

I looked around, taking in the vibrant chaos of Dave & Buster's before turning my attention back to Alex. "So, have you been here before?" I asked, trying to break the ice.

"Yeah, a couple of times," Alex replied, smiling. "I usually come here with my friends. What about you?"

"This is actually my first time," I admitted, glancing around again. "It's a lot more lively than I expected."

Alex chuckled. "Yeah, it can be pretty overwhelming at first, but it's a lot of fun once you get into it. Do you have a favorite game so far?"

"I enjoyed the air hockey table a lot. Especially beating you was fun," I said.

He blushed for a second.

"I kinda suck at it if I'm being honest. We can have a rematch if you want," he said.

"We should. Are you sure about that?" I asked in a playful tone.

"Oh, I'm not going to let you win a second time," he said.

I smiled and took one of my chicken tenders, dipping it into some barbecue sauce. Alex took a sip of his margarita.

"I wanted to talk to you about something. We're having a gallery auction event at the end of the month at the studio, and I think you should submit a painting. It's going to be an event where locals can come and bid on each art piece. All the proceeds go directly to the artists since so many talented people aren't making enough money from their art. It's a way for us to keep promoting art as something of value in our society. What do you think?" he asked.

"That sounds amazing, but I don't know. I don't think I'm good enough yet," I said.

"Yes, you are. I've seen your work. That's why I'm asking you. Like I told you before, I've seen what you can create, and I think it's a great opportunity for people to discover your work. It's just one canvas, so no pressure. If you don't want to do it, you don't have to be part of the auction. You can come just to support the event," he said.

"Does the painting have to be about a specific topic?" I asked.

"Yes! The theme for the event is The Celestial Garden. You can interpret the theme however you like in your painting. The team decided that the event is going to be like a flower garden under the stars," he said.

"That's a beautiful theme," I said.

"We're going to have a cocktail party, and it's going to be like a small gala event. Are you up for the challenge?" he asked.

"Count me in. I'm kinda nervous, but I have nothing to lose," I said.

"I'm absolutely sure you are going to create something special," he said. "You have to try these Cantina Nachos," he added, handing me his plate.

"That's really good. Mexican food is so good," I said.

"You mean the white version of Mexican food?" Alex said.

"There's no doubt the authentic version has to be way better," I said.

"Oh, that's not even to be questioned," he said.

"What do you usually like to do in your free time?" I asked.

"I really enjoy traveling. I usually go out of the country twice a year. Last year I visited Japan for the first time, and it was one of the best experiences I ever had. I want to go back, but I have a lot of countries I want to check off my list," he replied.

"How many countries have you visited?" I asked.

"Around nine, if my memory doesn't fail me," he said.

"That's so nice. I have never stepped outside the country," I said.

"What?" he said.

"I know, right? That is something I would eventually like to do at some point in my life," I said.

"When I'm not traveling, I enjoy reading," he said.

"Another fellow bookworm. What are you currently reading?" I asked.

"I'm reading a fantasy novel based on Dungeons and Dragons. It's called Kingdom of Fire by Clark Thompson. It's really good. I'm kind of a nerd when it comes to books," he said.

"The fantasy novels and you loving to travel makes me think that you're quite adventurous," I said.

"I would say that's pretty accurate. What about you? What do you typically read? Let me guess, romance," he said.

"I do love my comfort romance. I love how character-focused they are, but I read pretty much anything fiction. I like to dabble in every genre," I said.

"Spicy romance?" he asked.

"Not my thing. But you're familiar with the term, so I assume you've read a few of them," I said.

"Like two of them, if I'm being honest," he said.

"Why are you turning red?" I said, smiling. "There's nothing wrong with being a hopeless romantic. Oh no, even your ears are turning red."

"I think the tequila shot is finally catching up to me," he said.

His whole face turned pink, and I couldn't hold my laugh.

"No, I get it. That's how you know the spice level of a romance," I said.

"By having a reaction like mine? You're making me sweat," he said, airing out his shirt.

"Are you okay?" I asked.

"No, I'm good," he said.

"Should we look for Emily? I'm trying to see if I can spot her from here, but I don't see her anywhere. I'm getting a little worried," I said.

"Let's go find her," Alex said.

"I just want to check if she's okay," I said.

We immediately headed toward the bar, but she wasn't there. There were a group of people sitting at the bar drinking, but no Emily to be seen. I got nervous for a second. I know she's an adult, but disappearing with a man she just met worries me. We went straight to the arcade area and checked aisle by aisle but found nothing.

"Where could she possibly be?" I asked Alex.

"Text her, maybe she is in the bathroom," Alex said.

"Hey Emily. Where are you? We are looking for you," I texted.

We went back to our table to wait for her response, and a few minutes passed by without any reply. Alex looked for her at the bar again, but she wasn't there.

"Maybe she's outside," Alex said.

We hurried to the parking lot and immediately saw Emily laughing with the guy she had just met next to what seemed like his car.

"Emily, we've been looking for you for the past twenty minutes," I said.

"Oh girl, I'm fine. Come meet my new friend Dave from Dave & Buster's! Isn't that hilarious? He's like the king of this place," she said.

She clearly was not fine. Her facial expressions looked way different from the Emily I know. I think she had a little too much to drink.

"Hi Dave! Emily, it's time to go home. You said you were going to help me with some stuff at my house," I said.

"What stuff?" she asked.

"Don't you remember the shower curtain you told me you were going to help me put up?" I said.

"It's almost midnight," Dave said.

"Yeah, we have been super busy these days," I said.

"Thank you for keeping her entertained, but we really need to get her home," Alex said.

"Bye babe. Call me!" Emily said as we walked back to Alex's car.

"Oh my god, you guys. You are both such cock-blockers. I think he was the love of my life," she said, looking frustrated.

Emily was clearly drunk.

"How many drinks did you have?" Alex asked.

"A few. It was the five-dollar happy hour special. It's fine. I'm fine. I still can't believe how hot my Dave was," she said, putting her hand on her forehead.

Emily started walking in front of us, taking her shoes off and walking barefoot on the extremely dirty parking lot. I don't know what happened to her hair, but it looked like it had been through some rough stuff.

"Are you going to open up the spaceship for me?" she said.

"You mean my Tesla?" Alex said.

"Same thing. Are we off to Mars?" Emily said.

"No, we are going to take you home," Alex said.

"Is Elon going to be there?" she asked.

"I don't think so," Alex said.

"So you're telling me this battery-operated golf cart can't take us to Mars?" she said, annoyed.

"Not yet," he responded.

I was concerned about Emily, but the things coming out of her mouth made me laugh. I was trying hard to hold it in and focus on helping her out. We safely got her inside the car.

"Alexa, play 'Nasty' by Tinashe!" Emily yelled.

"Tesla doesn't have Alexa," Alex said.

"Are you kidding me? No Tinashe!" she said.

"I can totally play the song for you, just not with an Alexa command," Alex said.

"You heard it here first. Elon doesn't fuck with Alexa. Isn't that strange? Doesn't he have like twelve kids?" Emily said.

Alex couldn't hold it together.

"Is somebody gonna match my freak? Is somebody gonna match my nasty? I got stamina, they say I'm an athlete," Emily started singing out loud. "The seat belt is not letting me twerk," Emily said.

"That's okay. You can twerk when we get home. Please keep your seatbelt on," I said, looking back at her.

"You guys are so boring. You make a cute couple, though. Boring people tend to attract each other," she said.

"We are not boring," Alex said.

"I have a boyfriend," I said.

"Yes, you are. You don't even use the self-driving feature on this spaceship," she said.

"Oh, I didn't pay extra for that feature," Alex said.

"Proves my point. Boring!" she said.

"I think I'm going to let Emily sleep at my place. We can't leave her alone at her apartment like this," I said to Alex.

"No, absolutely," Alex said.

"Emily, you're going to stay with me tonight at my house," I said loudly so she could hear me.

"A slumber party?" she asked.

"Kind of," I replied.

"What about Alex?" Emily said.

"I'm going to my place," Alex said.

"You don't want to stay with us for our late-night gossip?" Emily said, annoyed at his response.

"No, I'm good," he said.

"Well, your loss. No tea for you," she said.

All of a sudden, Emily finally stopped talking. She passed out in the car.

We parked in my parents' driveway. It was extremely quiet as always, but at one in the morning, you could hear a pin drop.

"Emily, we are home," I said, waking her up.

"Ugh, I'm not feeling that great. I feel like I'm going to puke," Emily said, looking pale as a ghost.

"Here, I have a plastic bag," Alex said, grabbing a plastic bag from under his seat.

The barfing sound made us concerned for her. She started crying out of nowhere.

"What's wrong?" I asked, worried about her state.

"I'm not drinking ever again. I didn't even go home with Buster," Emily said, as she exhaled a breath that almost burned our eyebrows off.

"You mean Dave?" I said.

"Same thing. Did you see how hot he was?" Emily said.

"Not personally my type, but I totally understand your frustration. You're going to be alright. Don't worry about it. You won't even remember anything by tomorrow," I said.

"Come on, Emily, let us help you take a shower so you feel better," Alex said, trying to look slightly into the back seat.

"Excuse me! I'M NOT GETTING NAKED IN FRONT OF YOU," she said out loud.

"That's not what I meant. Madison is going to help you out in case you need anything," Alex said.

Helping Emily get into the shower was a challenge, but thankfully, we made it through. I let her use some of my pajamas. Alex waited for us, sitting by my bedroom door. He made sure to offer his hand in case we needed help, and we did. Emily made him carry her to bed like they were on their honeymoon. After finally tucking Emily in, I thanked Alex for his help.

"If you need anything, make sure to call me. Here's my number. I'm going to keep my phone on for the rest of the night," he said.

"Thank you for your help," I said.

"No problem," he said as he gave me a kiss on the cheek.

"Good night," he said.

"Good night to you too," I said as I closed the front door.

I lay next to Emily in bed, making sure not to wake her up. I stared straight at the ceiling, letting out a huge sigh of relief.

"Dave!" Emily said.

# Chapter 17

# This Is Your Time

"What a chaotic night we had. Are you sure you don't remember most of it?" I asked.

"Not at all. The last thing I clearly remember is my conversation with Dave at the bar," Emily said, sitting next to me on my bed.

"Oh, you were all over him. What was that all about?" I mentioned.

"I don't know either. Being single for so long makes you do strange things. I guess I was entertained by the idea that someone wanted to give me some attention," she admitted.

"But did you have anything in common with him?" I asked.

"Not a single thing. He's such a player. That's something I hate in men," she said.

"Did you know you almost went home with him?" I said.

"Did I?" she asked.

"Yes! You were really mad at us because we prevented you from having sex with him. You were about to get in a car with a complete stranger while you were completely intoxicated. That's scary," I commented.

"Really? That's funny and embarrassing," she admitted.

"You can't drink like that if you're going to blackout and not remember anything," I said, concerned.

"Thank you for having my back. You're a real friend," she said, giving me a hug.

"What did Alex think about the whole situation?" she asked.

"I have never seen someone laugh as much as he did last night. You said the most unhinged thing to him," I said.

"Oh no," she said.

"It's okay. I think he handled everything with a positive attitude. Yesterday, I saw that he's genuinely a great guy and a good friend too," I said.

We went straight to the kitchen where my mom was making waffles for breakfast.

"Mom, this is Emily, my friend from the art workshop. Emily, this is Heather, my mom," I said.

"Nice to meet you, Emily," Mom said.

"Nice to meet you too, Mrs. Heather," Emily said.

"Are you going to stay for some waffles?" Mom asked.

"I would love to," Emily responded.

"Mom, sorry that I didn't tell you Emily was staying over since you were sleeping," I said.

"Oh, don't worry about it. I told you before that you're always welcome to bring friends over when you like. I don't have a problem with that," Mom said.

"Thanks, Mom," I said.

We sat at the dining room table for breakfast. Mom got to know more about Emily, asking her the usual small talk questions you go over when meeting someone for the first time. After our long conversation, Emily called an Uber to pick up her car at the shopping plaza.

"Good morning, babe!" I texted Benson.

"Good morning, my love. What are you up to?" he texted back.

I shared my last night's adventure with Emily and Alex, told him about the Celestial Garden gala, and mentioned that we both needed outfits for the event.

"We should go thrift shopping for our outfits," I suggested.

"Are you sure? We can go to the mall," he responded.

"The mall is too far, and besides, I've been wanting to go thrift shopping for a long time," I wrote.

"You want to go today? I'm free today. It could be a fun date," he wrote.

"Yeah, let's do it. We should go for ice cream afterward. It's a perfect summer day for a chocolate ice cream cone," I texted.

"Yum. I'll pick you up at 1:30 p.m. And by the way, you owe me a kiss for each day that has passed without me seeing you," he texted.

"No, I can't. I'm having garlic bread for lunch," I joked.

"No, you're not," he said.

"I am," I texted while smiling.

"Aw," he said.

"Why do you sound so disappointed?" I asked.

"I just wanted to give you a little smooch," he texted.

"I love you. Just know that I will love you even with garlic breath," I admitted.

"You liar," he replied.

"It's true. I will love you with all your imperfections. All of them," I said.

"I wish you could smell my shirt after a run to see if you change your mind about that," he wrote.

"Eww, Ben! From garlic to onions," I joked.

"That's true love. I love you," he said.

"I love you too," I responded.

"Are we going to make out through the phone?" he asked.

"Go for it and let me know how it goes," I replied.

"Hahaha," he texted.

"I'm going to sadly let you go. I'm gonna start getting ready," I wrote.

"Why? Don't leave me," he texted.

"I can't. I get distracted," I texted back.

"Talk to you in a few hours then. Love you!" he said.

"Love you too," I said.

I heard a knock on our front door. "It's Ben," I said to Mom. As I swung the door open, Ben was standing on our front porch, looking handsome as always for our date. He wore cream shorts, a vertical striped shirt, and white sneakers. He was holding a bouquet of flowers.

"These are for you," he said.

"Ben! That's so sweet. Thank you!" I said, giving him a hug and a kiss.

I took a look at the flowers, and it was a beautiful arrangement. It had purple daisies with some white wildflowers. Nestled between each flower were a few sprigs of baby's breath, giving the arrangement a whimsical look.

"Come inside. I'm going to put them in water before we leave," I said.

Mom was making lunch in the kitchen.

"Hi, Ben! How are you?" Mom asked.

"I'm good. How are you?" he said as he hugged Mom.

"I'm doing great. Oh my god, what a beautiful bouquet of flowers," she said. "That's so romantic. Ben, you get a few points for that. Do you know how long it's been since your father bought me flowers?"

"Mother's Day," I mentioned.

"Exactly! That was like two months ago," she said while opening a kitchen cabinet. "Here. I got the perfect vase for them. As soon as I finish preparing my lunch, I can cut the stems for you since you're going out."

"Are you sure? I can do it before we head out," I said.

"Yeah, absolutely. I got time. You guys go and have fun," she said.

"Thanks, Mom," I said.

"Where are you guys going?" she asked.

"I'm going to try to find a dress for the gallery auction at the thrift store," I replied.

"After that, we are getting some ice cream," Benson said.

"And I didn't get invited to these fun activities?" she joked.

"You can be our third wheel if you want," I said.

"No. I'll let you guys share your ice cream together. Although ice cream does sound really good right now," she said.

"Next time we have to invite you over when we go out," Ben said.

"Oh, absolutely. I am craving some Korean barbecue food, to give you guys any ideas," Mom said.

"There's a restaurant near the east downtown mall that we can go to someday," Ben suggested.

"So there you go. We have some future plans. We are going to go. Mom, if you want to, I can really put the flowers in the vase when I return," I said.

"No, I got it. You guys go have some fun and at least take a picture of the ice cream shop menu to see the different flavors they have. James and I are always looking for new places to visit," she said.

"Yeah, I can do that for you. We are going to go now. See you later!" I said.

"Bye, Ben! Don't let Maddie pick an ugly dress," she said.

Ben laughed.

"I will try my best. I'll let you know how it goes," Ben said.

"Mom, don't forget to lock the door," I said, as Ben closed the front door.

"I love that your mom always has an uplifting spirit," Ben said.

"She's like that 24/7. Dad is the more reserved one in the house. I get to experience both personalities and I have learned to appreciate them both equally. They balance each other out pretty well," I said.

"That's going to be me and you in the future," Ben said.

"I don't talk as much as my mom does. She could have a conversation with a wall. I'm very socially anxious, but once I open up to someone, that's when I truly don't shut up," I said.

"What are we going to do then if I also don't talk a lot?" he asked.

"Enjoy our company. The best company is the one where you can sit in silence and know that their presence is just enough," I said.

"And why don't I feel that in a waiting room with strangers?" he asked.

"I feel it. I feel respect for the other people around me. That's why we let them have their space," I said.

"Okay, Maya Angelou," he said.

"I love her. I have a quote of hers on a sticky note on my laptop," I said.

"And what does it say?" he asked.

"It says, 'I can be changed by what happens to me. But I refuse to be reduced by it.' I see it almost every day and it has had a profound meaning in my life since I became paralyzed," I responded.

"How do you know Maya's work?" I asked as we got inside the car.

"I read her book I *Know Why The Caged Bird Sings* about two years ago, and it was life-changing. Her struggles growing up and the lessons she learned as a woman of color were incredible to hear. I think those are the voices we should hear on a daily basis," he said.

"You are right. Now that I'm disabled, my whole perspective on life has changed drastically. Underrepresented communities like mine need spaces to be heard. Especially nowadays when everyone has a microphone with nothing important to say," I said.

"You should write a book," he joked.

"Maybe someday. But what happens if it flops?" I asked.

"At least you tried to put your voice out there. Maybe the right people will find it eventually," Ben said.

We gazed into each other's eyes and smiled. Ben gently took my hand, and our fingers intertwined, becoming one. In that moment, it felt as though our souls were connected, sharing an unspoken bond that transcended words.

We walked hand in hand arriving at the charming storefront of ReLove It. The sign, adorned with a heart and a vintage font, invited us inside with promises of hidden gems and unique finds. The bell above the door jingled softly as we entered, and the comforting scent of aged wood and old leather greeted us.

Inside, ReLove It was a treasure trove of eclectic styles and eras, each section carefully curated to tell a story. My eyes sparkled with excitement as Ben gravitated toward the racks of clothing, each one a journey through time.

The first section we explored was the vintage collection, where rich velvet dresses from the

'60s hung next to tailored suits from the '50s. The colors ranged from deep, royal purples to vibrant, cheerful yellows, each garment exuding a sense of history and elegance. I ran my fingers over the delicate lace of a Victorian blouse, imagining the life it once lived.

Moving deeper into the store, I discovered the casual wear section, a delightful array of faded denim jackets, well-worn band t-shirts, and cozy flannel shirts. The shelves were lined with perfectly broken-in jeans, their soft fabric bearing the marks of many adventures. Benson picked up a leather jacket, its rugged charm and subtle scuffs telling tales of road trips and rebellious escapades.

ReLove It also boasted a remarkable collection of accessories. A wall dedicated to hats displayed everything from wide-brimmed fedoras to knitted beanies, each piece adding a touch of personality to any outfit. Nearby, a glass case showcased an assortment of vintage jewelry—brooches, necklaces, and rings sparkling under the soft lighting.

In the corner, a display of eclectic footwear caught my eye. Rows of polished leather boots, colorful sneakers, and elegant heels were neatly arranged, waiting for new owners to step into their stories. Benson admired a pair of sturdy hiking boots, imagining future trails he could conquer.

As we wandered through the store, Benson and I were drawn to the creative repurposing section. Here, old garments had been transformed into new, innovative pieces. A denim jacket embellished with intricate embroidery, a skirt made from repurposed ties, and handbags crafted from vintage fabric scraps showcased the artistry and sustainable spirit of the thrift store.

Every corner of ReLove It held a new surprise, variety and charm of the clothing on offer. From formal wear to casual attire, each item was a unique piece waiting to be rediscovered and loved anew. Our hearts swelled with the thrill of the hunt, the promise of finding something truly special amid the racks and shelves of our now new favorite thrift store.

"Ben, you have to try these on," I said as I found a cowboy hat and a pair of men's cowboy boots.

"No way! I'm going to look like Woody from Toy Story," he said.

"Please! Let's find you some straight-leg jeans and a T-shirt. Look, they even have a cowboy-looking belt," I said, examining the guitar-shaped silver buckle of a brown leather belt.

"You're a little too excited about this," he said.

"I promise I'm going to make you look good. Let me live my real-life cowboy romance novel for a few minutes," I said.

We found a plain black T-shirt and a pair of medium-wash denim jeans.

"These will work. Let's find the dressing room," I said as I looked around.

"You're going to make me try this on here," he said.

"That's the whole point," I said.

"Aren't we supposed to be looking for your dress?" he asked.

"We have time," I said, holding back my laughter.

"Fine. I'm doing this just because I love you," he said as he closed the dressing room curtain.

"Babe, I think these jeans are a little too tight on my legs. No, no, no, no. I can't walk out like this," he said, laughing.

"You're fine. Make sure to put the hat on," I said.

"I don't even know if this thing is backwards. Are you ready?" he asked.

"I'm ready," I responded.

"Yee-haw!" he said as he dramatically pulled back the curtain.

I immediately started laughing.

"Save a horse, ride a cowboy," I said.

"Shhh! You can't say that out loud," Ben said.

"Sorry. Wait! Why do you look so good in those jeans? Turn around. Your butt is bigger than mine," I said.

"Oh! I don't skip leg day at the gym," he said, looking at his thighs.

"This should be your everyday outfit," I said.

"There's no chance I will wear something like this again," he said.

"Are you sure? You look like a hottie in that outfit," I said.

"I look like I'm about to give you a striptease," he said.

"Maybe you should," I joked.

"Hey! Are you okay? Is the summer heat getting to you?" he said, touching my forehead.

He put both hands on his belt and said, "This ain't Texas, woo!" while moving his hips in a circle.

We laughed.

"Okay, I'm done," he said, going back to the stall.

"They're going to kick us out," I said.

"For looking this good?" he said.

"No, for being loud," I said.

"No more role-playing. Let's find your dress," he said as he walked out of the dressing room. "What type of dress are you looking for?"

"I have no idea. Whatever catches my eye. Maybe something floral or spring-like since the theme is a play on a garden," I suggested.

We looked through the women's formal racks and passed a lot of vibrant neon-colored cocktail dresses. Benson pulled the hangers one by one so I could take a complete look at them. I ended up liking a short, strappy black dress but decided it was not formal enough. Then, as we passed through some floral maxi dresses, a beautiful pink floral-detailed ball gown took my breath away.

"That one is perfect! It's beautiful," I said, touching the sheer pink fabric.

I tried it on. I needed a little assistance from Ben since it was a long dress. I walked out to take a look at a bigger mirror outside the dressing room.

"You look stunning! Do I have the most beautiful girlfriend on this planet?" he said.

"Oh, stop!" I said.

"You are," he said.

"I don't even know how to describe it. I've never seen something like it before," I said.

"The dress has a paper tag on the back with a paragraph description of it," Ben said.

"Do you want to read it for me?" I asked.

"Let me see," he said. "The dress is a stunning light pink ball gown, featuring a fitted bodice with a classic square neckline and short, delicately adorned sleeves. The fabric is ethereal and airy, cascading into a voluminous skirt layered with sheer, pastel floral embellishments. Intricate embroidery and appliqué techniques create a three-dimensional effect, making the flowers appear to bloom across the gown. The waste line is subtly defined, enhancing the natural curves and transitioning gracefully into the flowing skirt. This dress evokes a fairy-tale charm, reminiscent of a blooming garden, with its harmonious blend of pink hues and romantic floral motifs."

"Wow. I would never be able to describe it like that. Could it be more perfect for the Celestial Garden theme?" I said.

"I'm wondering why someone would donate a dress like that," he said.

"Right! But where would you wear something like this?" I asked.

"Oh, easy. If I were a woman, I'd be picking up my mail in that thing. To the gym, running errands. The options are endless," he said.

"Has anyone ever told you that you're actually funny?" I said, smiling.

"I don't think so. You just bring out the best in me," he said.

I gave him a side hug. We went to the cash registry, I paid for my dress and we headed out to the ice cream shop.

I looked through the windshield and got excited when I saw the ice cream shop. Light pink brick walls, outdoor white tables and brown patio umbrellas made the neapolitan colors scheme stand out from the rest of the businesses. As we entered through the door to The Ice Cream Parlor, a wave of sweet, creamy aromas wafted over me, instantly making my mouth water. I squeezed Ben's hand, grinning as I took in the whimsical surroundings.

The entire shop was a delightful explosion of light pink. The walls were painted a soothing pastel pink, adorned with vintage ice cream posters and strings of fairy lights that twinkle like stars. Pink and white checkered tablecloths covered the small round tables, each topped with a tiny vase of fresh daisies. Even the counter, where an array of colorful ice cream tubs was displayed, was trimmed with delicate lace and dotted with jars of sprinkles and toppings.

We made our way to the counter, our footsteps echoing softly on the polished wooden floor. The girl behind the counter greeted us with a bright smile, her apron matching the pink theme. "Welcome to The Ice Cream Parlor! What can I get for you two today?"

Ben looked at me, his eyes sparkling with mischief. "Ladies first," he said, gesturing grandly. I laughed and rolled forward, my eyes scanning the myriad of flavors.

"I'll have a scoop of the Strawberry Dream and a scoop of Chocolate Magic, please," I said, already imagining the cool, creamy texture on my tongue.

"And for you, sir?" the girl asked, turning to Ben.

"I'll go with the Chocolate Bliss and the Caramel Swirl," he replied, his enthusiasm mirroring mine.

As we waited for our cones, I took another look around. Everything felt so cozy and inviting. The soft pink hues made it seem like we had stepped into a fairy tale. I could hear the faint sound of an old jazz tune playing in the background, adding to the charming ambiance.

When our ice cream was ready, we took our cones and found a small table by the window. Sitting across from Ben, I felt a warmth spread through me that had nothing to do with the ice cream. This place, with its enchanting decor and delicious treats, was perfect.

Ben took a bite of his Chocolate Bliss and sighed contentedly. "This is amazing," he said, his eyes meeting mine.

I smiled, taking my own bite. The flavors were rich and refreshing, exactly as I had hoped. "I love this place," I said, feeling a rush of happiness. "We should come here more often."

"Definitely," Ben agreed, his hand finding mine across the table.

We clinked our cones together like glasses of champagne, and I couldn't help but laugh. In this pink-hued wonderland, everything felt just right.

"Can I try yours?" I asked, my curiosity piqued as he stretched his ice cream cone toward me. I took a small bite.

"That is really good. I really like the caramel," I said, savoring the rich flavor.

"You got ice cream on the tip of your nose," he laughed, gently wiping it off with a paper napkin.

"Thanks! Want to try mine?" I offered.

"I really want to try the strawberry part," he said, taking a bite. "That's amazing! The real strawberry chunks make it a ten out of ten."

"I can see myself doing stuff like this with you for the rest of my life," I said, a warmth spreading through me.

"Forever?" he asked, his eyes searching mine.

"Forever. I enjoy your company a lot. You make my days better," I confessed.

"I feel the same about you," he replied softly.

"I'm starting to believe you came into my life for a reason," I said.

"Why is that?" he asked, genuinely curious.

"I was at my lowest point when I met you. If it wasn't for that, our paths might never have crossed. What were the chances of us meeting that day? Imagine missing out on knowing you. There are people out there who are never going to get a chance to know you. Isn't that crazy?" I said.

"It is, now that I think about it like that," he agreed.

"I'm glad you're in my life. I don't often tell the people I love how I truly feel. I usually express it with my actions, but I'm trying to tell them more often since life is so short. Having Dylan on the back of my mind has taught me a lot about life in general," I said.

"How was he as a person?" he asked.

"The best friend anyone could ask for. He always made sure everyone around him felt seen. He accepted everyone for who they were, and he made a huge impact on my life. He was very special to me," I said.

"Do you have or had someone who made an impact like that in your life?" I asked.

"My grandparents on my mom's side of the family. They were the most loving people I know. Growing up, my grandma used to cook for us and ask us a thousand times if we had eaten. She always made sure we had everything we needed. My grandpa taught us to be more independent. He was the one who showed me how to tie my shoes. Those small things I took for granted are now cherished memories. It's crazy how we learn to appreciate people when they're no longer around," he said. "I guess we're all guilty of not focusing on the present," he said.

I nodded.

"Speaking of which, remember your mom requested a picture of the menu? It's been sitting in front of us this whole time," he said, raising a laminated menu from the table.

I quickly took a picture to send to my mom later. Just then, a woman walked by with her dog.

"Look at that cute dog! That's the cutest thing I've ever seen," I exclaimed.

"Are you a dog person or a cat person?" he asked.

"A dog person. I don't like cats," I admitted.

"What? Why?" he asked.

"They're so unpredictable. I don't like that," I said.

"But I love cats," he said.

"I can appreciate the tranquility they bring to a home," I said.

"They do have a calm presence about them. But dogs are pretty amazing, too. I'm not going to lie," he said.

"Tell me why every time I see a cat walking around a kitchen countertop, it makes me want to rip my hair out. That should be illegal," I said.

He laughed.

"They're cleaner than you think," he said.

"The jumping around like they're in a wild jungle isn't my thing either. Why are you laughing? It's true," I said.

"A jungle. Speaking your mind today?" he said.

"It's probably the sugar. I can feel it," I said.

A silence invaded our space. We could hear other people's conversations as background noise. I ate the cone part of my ice cream. The crunchiness of the cone mixed with the creamy consistency made the last bites the best ones.

"Is there a quirky habit you have that I don't know about yet?" he asked.

"I organize my books by color. Does that count? Having a color-coded bookshelf is aesthetically pleasing to my eyes," I said.

"I saw them when you showed me your room. That's a whole other level of being organized that I will never be," he said.

"I think you're already up there. Your apartment looks like something straight out of a Pottery Barn store," I said.

"Not even close," he said.

"Yes, it does. It looks like a showroom from a furniture store. A good one," I joked.

He smiled.

"Do you have any quirky habits I don't know about?" I asked.

"I break into spontaneous dances when I'm alone," he admitted, blushing a little.

"Like the one you did at the thrift store today?" I teased.

"They usually last longer than that," he said.

"Out of nowhere?" I asked.

"Yeah. I feel so much better after doing it. It's like a stress relief for me," he said, smiling.

"That would make anyone's life instantly better, to be honest," I said.

I smiled, appreciating his openness.

We talked for a while. While having our conversation, I noticed the subtle details in his facial expressions. How when he laughs you can barely see his eyes. His dimples are like little pockets of sunshine on his face, adding an extra dose of charm and sweetness to his smile. His lips are like a perfect blend of strength and softness, inviting and captivating with every smile. I got lost in his eyes. I really did.

"I had a blast with you today," I said as we walked to Ben's car, leaving the ice cream shop.

Ben rested his back against the passenger side of his car, keys in hand. He started fidgeting with them, looking nervous.

"Me too!" he said. "I want to tell you something."

"Is everything alright?" I asked, noticing a change in his demeanor.

"What are your thoughts on me moving to Norway?" he asked.

"You're moving to Norway?" I said, surprised and confused.

"I got accepted to study at a college in Norway," he said.

"Since when?" I asked.

"I got the letter through my email two days ago," he said. "I didn't know how you would react to the news."

When he told me he was possibly moving to another country, my heart shattered into a million pieces. I wanted to beg him to stay, but I knew I couldn't be that selfish. I plastered on a smile, congratulating him on this amazing opportunity, while inside, I felt like I was falling apart. The thought of not seeing him every day, of not being able to hold him, was unbearable. But I love him too much to stand in his way. So, I swallowed my heartache, nodding supportively, even though it felt like my world was ending.

"This is your time to go after your dreams," I said, getting a little teary-eyed.

He gave me a warm, enveloping hug, and as I nestled my head against his chest, I could feel the steady rhythm of his heartbeat, a comforting and familiar cadence. The subtle, woody notes of his sandalwood cologne surrounded me, creating a blend of safety and comfort. At that moment, the world seemed to pause, and I found myself wishing that time could stand still. I didn't want to let go of him, not now, not ever.

"We are going to make this work. I promise," he whispered.

# Chapter 18
## Celebrating Art

Sitting in front of my easel, I took a deep breath, feeling the weight of the brush in my hand. The canvas before me was a pristine expanse of white, waiting to be transformed. My vision for this painting was clear: to portray the diversity of flowers as a metaphor for the beauty of our differences.

I started with the background, using broad strokes of a warm, golden hue to create a luminous, inviting light. This light would be the unifying force, the sun that nourishes all blooms equally, regardless of their form or color. As the background dried, I mixed my palette, selecting vibrant reds, deep purples, soft pinks, and sunny yellows, each color representing a different flower, a different facet of human diversity.

I began with a rose, its petals unfolding gracefully in a bold crimson. The rose, often seen as the epitome of beauty, stood proudly on one side of the canvas. Its delicate petals and thorny stem were a reminder of strength and vulnerability intertwined.

Next, I turned my attention to the orchid. Its exotic and intricate shape, painted in shades of purple and white, spoke of uniqueness and rarity. The orchid seemed to float, its roots not confined to the earth but rather suspended, symbolizing those who find their place in the world despite challenges.

Beside the orchid, I painted a cluster of cherry blossoms, their pale pink petals soft and ephemeral. These flowers represented the fleeting moments of beauty and the delicate nature of life. They reminded me of the shared experiences that bind us together, even if only for a brief season.

On the other side of the canvas, a lily emerged. Its white petals, touched with hints of orange and gold, radiated purity and elegance. The lily's strong, straight stem stood as a testament to resilience and grace under pressure.

Finally, I added tulips, their bright, cheerful blooms in a rainbow of colors. Each tulip, distinct in its hue but similar in form, symbolized the joy found in diversity. Together, they created a sense of harmony and celebration.

As I stepped back, I felt a sense of fulfillment. Each flower, with its unique beauty and character, contributed to the whole, creating a vibrant and harmonious garden. This was my interpretation of humanity: a tapestry of differences that, when brought together, created something truly magnificent.

The painting was not just a collection of flowers but a statement. It whispered that our individuality is not something to be feared but celebrated, for it is our differences that make us beautiful. And in this celestial garden, every bloom, every petal, had a place and a purpose.

My mom walked into my bedroom, taking a look at my canvas.

"Oh, Madison! This has to be your best work yet. I don't even know where to focus my attention. Look at the cherry blossoms. The level of detail in this painting is just incredible," she said.

"Do you think it's going to sell?" I asked.

"Oh, I have no doubts that it will. Are you sure you want it to be auctioned?" she said.

"That's why I worked so hard on it. I wanted to create something special," I said.

"I can buy it from you," she said.

"I can make another one for you, if you want. It's going to take me two more weeks, though, and hours upon hours to complete," I said.

"It won't be the same. You have something really special here," she said as she sat on the side of the bed.

"Madison, I'm very proud of you. The way you've handled your life for the past few months has reminded me of how tough you are," she said.

"Thanks, Mom!" I said.

"Your dad and I have witnessed this crazy curveball that life threw at us, and seeing you handle it the way you have makes me so proud to be your mom," she said.

"Mom, you are going to make me cry," I admitted.

"Can you promise me that you are going to keep showing up for yourself every day for the rest of your life?" she said.

"Where are you going?" I questioned her, her words hitting me with uncertainty.

"Nowhere," she said.

"Why are you sounding so dramatic?" I asked.

"I just want to make sure that you always believe in yourself. Sometimes the world tries to convince us that we are not worthy. Don't ever let anyone tell you that you're not enough. That's all," she said.

"I promise," I said as she gave me a hug.

"Let me call your dad so he can see your masterpiece," she said.

The night of the gallery auction arrived. I stood in front of the mirror, my dress cascaded gracefully down to my ankles, the fabric swaying gently with my every movement. It was the perfect choice for tonight—elegant, yet vibrant, much like the painting I was about to unveil.

With a deep breath, I brushed a loose curl behind my ear. My hair had been styled into soft waves that framed my face. I smiled at my reflection, trying to calm the butterflies fluttering in my stomach. This was my night, a culmination of countless hours spent in my made shift studio in a corner of my room, pouring my heart and soul onto the canvas.

I stepped back to take in the full effect of my outfit. The gown's floral pattern seemed to come alive, the different shades of pink dancing across the fabric as if they were part of a living garden. It felt fitting, given the theme of my painting—an ode to the beauty and diversity of flowers, a celebration of differences.

I slipped into a pair of elegant, strappy heels, their subtle shimmer catching the light as I moved. The final touch was a pair of delicate earrings, thin silver earrings that dangled gracefully, echoing the theme of my gown. I gave myself one last, approving glance in the mirror before grabbing my clutch and heading towards the door.

I rolled out of the house to find Ben holding up a poster board that said, "I'm proud of you, babe!" in his own handwriting.

I couldn't stop smiling.

"Ben! You always go out of your way to make me smile. I love the sign," I said, giving him the biggest hug and a kiss.

"Look at you! Wow, simply wow. I'm speechless. You look really beautiful," he said.

"So do you! You look very handsome, and you smell really good," I said.

"Jeez, thanks!" he said.

"The sign took me back to my old high school days. I love it so much. This is going to be the highlight of my night," I said.

"I'm glad that it didn't go unnoticed," he said while smiling.

He stared into my eyes for a few seconds without saying anything.

"I can't believe how beautiful you are. I'm so lucky to have you in my life," he said.

"The feeling is mutual," I said.

We went inside the house where my parents were ready to go to the event.

"James!" Ben said, giving Dad a handshake and a hug.

"Nice! You look so dapper," Dad said.

"Look who's talking. Look at you! A true gentleman," Ben said, appreciating my dad's black tuxedo.

"Hi, Heather! You look beautiful. I brought you these," he said, giving Mom a kiss on the cheek and a bouquet of flowers.

"Oh, Benson, that's so sweet of you. Thank you! Are you guys excited for tonight?" Mom said.

"I'm a little nervous," I said.

"Don't be nervous. You got this!" Ben said.

"We're all going to be there to support you," Mom said.

"Did you see Maddie's painting?" Dad asked.

"No, I have not. Madison says she wants to surprise me at the event," Ben responded.

"Wait till you see it. It's a breathtaking piece," Mom said.

"Now I'm more nervous to show it to you with Mom hyping it up like that," I said.

"I know it has to be good. I've seen your previous work," Ben said.

"Imagine me revealing it to you, and it ends up being some stick-figure doodles," I said.

"I would hold my breath and still say that it looks good. It's the effort that counts," he said.

"Leonardo da Vinci would be screaming in the afterlife if he saw something like that. But you're not wrong. Anything can be art if you call it art," I said.

"It's all about how you introduce your art to the world," Mom said.

"I think it's about selling the idea of what's art. I would sell it like the sticks represent the simplicity of life or something like that. It's the representation of how fine life is," I joked.

"See! You don't have to worry about it. It's just art. It doesn't have to be that serious," Ben said.

"I've been practicing my interpretation of the painting for days. I think I've got how I'm going to explain it to people," I said.

"The Starry Night looks like a little kid painted it, and it's one of the most recognized pieces of art around the world. Don't put too much pressure on yourself. Just have fun tonight," Dad said.

"We have to take a picture of all of us together before we leave. That's my only request for the night," Mom said.

We all gathered around the living and took a group selfie. Seeing Alex fit so seamlessly into this dynamic filled me with a deep sense of happiness. My parents treated him like he was one of their own, and it was clear he felt comfortable and accepted. It was more than I had hoped for. I slipped my hand into his, giving it a squeeze. He looked at me, his eyes reflecting the warmth of the moment, and I knew then that he had found a place in my family's heart, just as they had in his.

As we stepped into the gallery, a sense of awe washed over me. The space had been transformed into a celestial garden, a realm where the ethereal and the earthly entwined. Soft, ambient music played, harmonizing with the gentle murmurs of the guests, creating a serene symphony that welcomed us.

The air shimmered with a delicate glow, as if sprinkled with stardust. Hanging from the ceiling were translucent orbs, each one resembling a miniature moon, casting a soft, silvery light. They swayed gently, as though moved by an invisible breeze, and their glow was mirrored in the polished floor, creating the illusion of walking on a path of stars.

The walls were adorned with intricate tapestries depicting scenes of cosmic beauty. Nebulae in vibrant hues of purple, blue, and pink blended seamlessly with verdant gardens, where flowers of unimaginable colors bloomed. Some pieces had been painted with luminescent paint, causing them to glow softly in the dim lighting, adding an otherworldly depth to the art.

Everywhere I looked, there were details that hinted at a deep, harmonious connection between the heavens and the earth. Tiny, delicate flowers with petals like spun silk hung from invisible threads, catching the light and casting delicate shadows on the walls.

The studio had been transformed into a sanctuary of serenity and wonder, a place where the boundaries of reality seemed to blur, and the beauty of the universe unfolded in all its splendor. As I wandered through the exhibit, my heart swelled with inspiration and a profound sense of peace.

"Alex! Oh my god. How? I can't even comprehend how beautiful everything turned out. This is out of this world," I said as I gave him a hug.

"Thank you! It took months and months of work. Everyone on the team worked countless hours to achieve this. I don't want to take all the credit. It was truly a team effort," he said.

"It shows. Everything looks incredible. Let me introduce you to my boyfriend Benson. Ben, this is Alex, my art instructor and friend," I said.

"Nice to meet you, Benson!" Alex said, extending his hand to Ben.

"Nice meeting you too! Congrats on everything," Ben said.

"Thank you!" Alex said.

"Madison, your painting is the fourth one on the left. I'm going to help with the cocktails. Feel free to come to the bar and grab some drinks whenever you want. See you around," Alex said.

Every painting was hung from the ceiling with this kind of fish wire that created the illusion of the canvases floating in the air. We faced my painting, and I soaked in Ben's facial expressions for a second.

"It's unreal. I'm taking it all in. I love the diverse flowers. Each one is so different from the others, but together they look beautiful," Ben said.

"You got my interpretation right. I'm so relieved. You just reassured me that my message is going to resonate with people," I said, holding his hand.

"You are so talented. It came out perfectly," he said as he leaned down to give me a kiss.

"Hi, Madison!" Emily said.

"Emily! Oh my gosh. You look stunning," I said.

"Look who's talking. That dress! Okay, supermodel," she said.

"Can you believe it's thrifted?" I said.

"Someone donated it? Girl, I need to go thrifting more often," she said.

"Benson, this is Emily! Emily, this is my boyfriend, Benson," I said.

"Nice to meet you, Benson!" she said as she hugged him.

"It's so nice to meet you too!" Ben said. "It was finally time that I met the guy who is dating this incredible woman," she said.

"Oh, stop!" I said.

"You are! Anyone is so lucky to have you in their life. You are the sweetest, most honest, and kindest person I know," she said.

Ben smiled.

"I'm going to grab us some drinks," Ben said.

I nodded.

"Do you want one?" Ben asked Emily.

"No, I'm good. I'm not drinking ever again, especially after our last outing. I'm going to be sober for the rest of my life, but thank you for asking," she responded.

"No problem," Ben said, walking away.

"Madison, why didn't you tell me you were dating a model? Look at him! Respectfully, he's beautiful. Girl, I'm so happy for you," she said.

"Thank you, he is pretty great," I said.

"I have such bad luck with men. That Dave from Dave & Buster's keeps hitting me up every day after I've told him for the hundredth time that I'm not interested. Some men are truly a nightmare," she said. "That's why water is going to be my drink of choice from now on."

"I'm pretty sure you are going to find your person when you least expect it," I said.

"No, I've learned my lesson. I'm going to keep focusing on myself. Who knows? Maybe my cat is my person. At least I don't need to hear my cat annoyed the shit out of me. My cat's companionship is more than enough for now," she said.

"I want to see your painting," I said.

"It's that one right there," she said as we moved closer to it.

"No, you didn't!" I said, laughing.

"Yes, I did!" she said.

Emily and I stood before a vibrant painting, its exaggerated figures and bright colors immediately catching my eye. Emily grinned and adopted a playful tour guide tone, clearly enjoying herself.

"This masterpiece is called 'The Garden of Masks,'" she began with a wink. "It's a satirical look at toxic masculinity, set in the most unexpected of places—a garden."

I raised my eyebrows, intrigued.

"At the center, behold the mighty Oak Man!" Emily declared. "He's tall and imposing, with broad shoulders and an iron mask that screams 'I'm too tough to feel feelings.' He's standing there like he's auditioning for a tree role in the next big fantasy movie. That mask? Purely for show. It's like he's hiding a secret stash of tissues for when no one's looking."

I couldn't help but giggle, completely entertained.

"To his right, meet Mr. Thorny Vines. He's all hunched over, looking like he's trying to untangle himself from a mess of social expectations. Poor guy's got these big thorny vines wrapped around him, probably thinking, 'Why can't I just wear pink and cry at rom-coms without being judged?'" Emily continued, her tone dripping with irony.

I laughed, feeling the amusement build.

"And over here, we have the Rose Bros," she said, pointing to a cluster of grinning men. "Look at them, all smiles on the outside, but trust me, those smiles hide some seriously prickly attitudes. They're like, 'Sure, I'm great! Never been better!' while secretly wondering if it's okay to admit they're scared of spiders."

I burst into laughter, thoroughly enjoying Emily's witty commentary.

"In the shadows back there, you'll see Sneaky Steve," Emily pointed to a barely visible figure behind a hedge. "He's the guy who's pretending everything's fine but secretly Googling 'why am I sad all the time?' when no one's watching. That hedge is his way of saying, 'I'm not coming out until toxic masculinity is cancelled.'"

I snorted, shaking my head at the clever depiction.

"And last but not least, we have Hope Flower," Emily said, gesturing to a small, delicate bloom at the garden's edge. "This little guy is here to remind everyone that, yes, even the most macho of men can bloom into emotionally intelligent beings. It's like he's saying, 'Come on, guys, it's okay to like puppies and rom-coms! Let's water our souls and grow!'"

I wiped away a tear of laughter. "Emily, this is hilarious! You've turned something so serious into pure comedy gold."

Emily grinned, clearly pleased with my reaction. "I figured humor was the best way to tackle such a heavy topic. Sometimes, a good laugh is all you need to start seeing things differently."

We shared a chuckle, appreciating the painting's witty take on the complexities of masculinity.

"Am I wrong? And that's it," she said.

"That's genius! You clearly put your feelings on that canvas," I said.

"Life imitates art far more than art imitates life, they say, or something like that. I'm not sure," she said.

"Bravo!" I said.

"Thank you! If I don't make a million for that tonight, I'm going back to drinking," she said.

"I love you. Thank you for always making me laugh," I said.

"Of course. That's why I'm here. I love you too. Thank you for accepting me for who I am. I'm going to grab a water bottle before I make another mistake," she said.

"What did I miss?" Ben said as he came back with our drinks.

"Take a look at Emily's painting," I said.

"That's really clever. It's a depiction of men," he said.

"It's a take on toxic masculinity seen from her perspective," I said.

"She seems like a fun, energetic person. You can even see it in her work. It's like seeing her personality plastered on a canvas," Ben said.

"She's truly the best. There's never a dull moment when you are around her," I said.

"Here, I brought you a Mai Tai. It has dark and white rum, freshly squeezed orange juice, lime juice, and I think he said orgeat syrup. I don't have a clue what that is," Ben said.

"It looks really summery with the pineapple wedge and the cherry on top. Let me try it," I said, taking a sip of the cocktail. "It has a slightly fruity taste but is very strong. It's not that bad!"

Ben took a sip of his drink.

"Oh, that's dangerous. Very strong. Yeah! I'm not sure if I like that," he said.

"Ben my man!" Alex said while putting his hand on Ben's shoulder. "What a lucky man you are."

Ben was clearly uncomfortable by his lack of personal space.

"Madison is such an incredible woman. You know if she was single I would probably ask her out," Alex said.

Ben tensed up, his jaw tightening as he forced a smile.

"Yeah, she is," he replied, trying to keep his voice steady. He gently shrugged Alex's hand off his shoulder, stepping back to create some distance.

Alex either didn't notice or didn't care about Ben's discomfort. "Man, you're really living the dream. She's smart, funny, and beautiful. You're one lucky guy."

Ben nodded, his patience wearing thin. "Thanks, Alex. I appreciate the compliment."

Alex grinned, seemingly oblivious to the growing tension. "So, what's your secret, huh? How'd you manage to snag someone like Madison?"

Ben took a deep breath, reminding himself to stay calm. "No secret, really. Just being myself and treating her with respect."

Alex laughed, patting Ben on the back again. "Respect, huh? I guess I should try that sometime."

Ben forced another smile, hoping the conversation would end soon. "Yeah, you should."

I was surprised to hear Alex talk like that.

"Catch you guys around. The auction is going to start really soon," Alex said.

Ben was clearly annoyed with the interaction.

"I didn't know I was competing for your love," he said as he drank more of his cocktail.

"You are not," I said.

"And what was that all about?" he said.

"I'm sorry that he made you feel that way. You know that I love you more than anything," I said.

"Don't be sorry. He told the truth. I am very lucky to have you. I just hate to admit that I'm kind of jealous. It's a hard pill to swallow. And for a second, I thought he was a cool guy," he said.

"Madison, all of your peers' work is incredible. Can you believe one of the paintings had real-life flower petals?" Mom said.

"Are you okay?" Dad said to Ben.

"Yeah! I'm fine. I'm having a great night so far," Ben said, taking another sip of his drink.

"Testing one, two, three. Testing, testing. Okay we are good to go. Good evening everyone! Hope that you are having a fantastic time so far. Please gather around and take a seat wherever you like. We are going to start our auction in a few minutes." The voice of Alex projected through the whole studio from a loudspeaker.

We took a seat way in the back because we didn't want to be too close to the front. The auction started, and Emily's painting was the first to go. You could hear the murmur of people talking about her modern take on masculinity. Her message was well received.

"Three hundred!" a man said in the crowd.

"Five hundred!" a woman proceeded with her offer.

"Anyone else? It's a painting with a strong statement," Alex said.

"Eight hundred!" a lady in her seventies shouted.

"Can we get higher than eight hundred? No? No one else? Sold to the sweet lady in red," Alex said.

Up next was my painting. The auction was buzzing with the energy of art enthusiasts and collectors. My heart pounded as I glanced at the painting displayed under the bright lights. It was my painting, a bold and vibrant representation of embracing diversity. Every brushstroke, every color choice was a part of me, and now it was about to go under the hammer.

"Up next a beautiful take on embracing diversity and finding beauty in each one of us, no matter how different we all may be." Alex said.

"That one is gorgeous." We heard a woman sitting in front of us say.

Immediately, hands shot up. My eyes widened. Five hundred! I nudged my dad, who was sitting next to me, grinning like the Cheshire Cat.

"Did you see that, Dad? Five hundred!" I whispered, trying to keep my voice steady.

He leaned in, whispering back, "Just you wait. Old Dad's got a few tricks up his sleeve."

The bid quickly rose to a thousand, then two. I couldn't believe it. My dad raised his paddle nonchalantly. "Five thousand!" he called out.

"Dad! What are you doing?" I hissed. We don't have that amount of money.

He gave me a wink. "Just having a little fun."

Alex pointed in our direction. "Five thousand, we have five thousand. Do I hear six thousand?"

Another bidder, a sleek woman in a black dress, raised her paddle. "seven thousand."

"Eight thousand!" Dad shouted, his competitive streak kicking in.

I covered my face with my hands. "Dad, please, you don't have to do this."

"Nonsense. This painting is priceless. Plus, your mother will kill me if I don't bring it home."

The room chuckled at my dad's antics, but the bids kept climbing. The stranger across the room, an elegant man with a mysterious air, entered the fray. "Ten thousand."

"Eleven!" Dad retorted without missing a beat.

"Twelve," the stranger said calmly, his eyes never leaving the painting.

I tugged at Dad's sleeve. "Dad, you're going to bankrupt us."

"Not if I sell my car," he muttered, eyes twinkling with mischief.

"Dad!"

"Thirteen thousand!" Dad's voice was triumphant.

"Fifteen thousand," the stranger said, and this time, he looked directly at my dad, a small smile playing on his lips.

I held my breath. This was it. My dad's paddle hovered, but before he could raise it, I grabbed his arm. "Dad, no. Seriously, it's okay."

He sighed, looking at me, then back at the stranger.

Alex gavel came down. "Sold! To the gentleman for fifteen thousand."

The room burst into applause. The stranger gave me a nod, a silent acknowledgment of my work. As the crowd began to disperse, Dad turned to me, eyes twinkling with pride.

"See? Now you know your old man would fight tooth and nail for your art. Even if I had to sell my car."

I laughed, hugging him. "Thanks, Dad. You're the best."

"Just promise me one thing," he said, squeezing my shoulders.

"Anything," I said.

"Next time, paint something cheaper," he said.

"You did it!" Alex said, giving me a hug. "I'm so proud of you."

"Congratulations! I told you it was an incredible piece. Give me a hug," Mom said.

"I promise I'm going to paint you a replica," I said in her ear.

"You don't have to. This is a gift in itself. Seeing you follow your passion is more than enough for me. I'm so proud of you. Remember what I promised you in that hospital bed, that I'm going to be by your side with each step you take in your life. I'm glad we got to experience this together," Mom said.

"Can I grab you for a few seconds?" Ben said.

Benson pulled me aside to a corner where there weren't too many people.

"Yesterday, I wrote you a letter since I'm not that good at expressing my feelings verbally. I thought I could say it better in written words," he said.

My awed expression was a side effect of my melted heart. He took a folded piece of paper out of his pocket and gave it to me. It read:

*Hey my love,*

*I just wanted to take a moment to tell you how incredibly proud I am of you. Watching you pour your heart and soul into everything you do is inspiring, and it reminds me every day of just how amazing you are.*

*You have this incredible ability to set your mind to something and make it happen, no matter the challenges. Your determination and passion are truly unmatched, and I know that you can achieve anything you set your mind to.*

*Keep shining, my love. The world is a better place with your talents and kindness in it.*

*With love,*

*Benson*

"That is so sweet. I love you," I said, giving him a kiss and a hug, resting my hand on the back of his head. Being close to him never gets old.

Today was absolutely amazing. I woke up to the warmth of the sun streaming through my window, and the day just got better from there. I spent the morning with my family, sharing laughter and stories over breakfast. The highlight of my day, though, celebrating my art with the people that I love. Their support and love always make me feel cherished and invincible. I am so incredibly grateful for the wonderful people in my life who make every day special. Today, especially, reminded me how lucky I am to have such an amazing family, friends, and boyfriend.

# Chapter 19
# Part of Me

A month has passed since the auction, and I'm taking my painting more seriously now. The night of the event was a pivotal moment in my life. I used to be so insecure about my ability to create incredible pieces of art that not only met my standards, but were also appreciated by others. It's interesting how confidence is something you gain only when you see the results of your progress. I have never felt so sure of what I want to do for the rest of my life.

Painting has taught me patience. Good things take time. That timeline between starting something new and arriving at the finish line is where the magic happens. I have learned to appreciate those moments, those in-between moments when you just want to give up. Those are the moments when true growth happens.

Painting has also helped me take my mind off things. It is still hard for me to accept that Ben is leaving today to study abroad. Every time I think about it, I want to cry. Why is it so hard to let go of the people we love? I want to be with him for the rest of my life. I knew it would be hard, but I never expected it to be this devastating. It feels like I'm letting a part of myself go. Fortunately, we have technology to keep in touch, but there is nothing like having the person you love next to you. That presence can't be transmitted through a screen. That human touch, as simple as a handshake, or those hugs that make you feel really close to the people you love, is irreplaceable. That is the hardest part of letting go of the people we love. I wish I could hold on to people forever, but sadly, life isn't like that.

"Are you ready?" Mom said.

"Almost. Let me grab my sweater real quick," I said.

We got in the car. We both put our seatbelts on.

"Did you text Ben that we are on our way?" mom said, as she pushed the start button of the car.

"I did. He's making sure that he's not leaving anything behind before we pick him up," I said.

"He still has plenty of time; his flight doesn't leave until three thirty in the afternoon," Mom said, as she reversed her way out of the driveway. "How are you feeling?"

"I can't even talk about it without getting all emotional," I said.

"That's okay. It's completely understandable. If I were in your position I would be reacting the same way," Mom said. "Remember that it is not like you are not ever going to see him again,"

"I know that's what I repeat myself a million times," I said.

Mom reached over and gave my hand a reassuring squeeze as she kept her eyes on the road. "You two have been close for so long. It's only natural to feel this way," she said.

I nodded, already tearing up, staring out the window as the familiar streets passed by. "It's just that everything is changing so quickly. First my accident, now this..." I said before getting choked up.

"Change is part of life, honey. It's what helps us grow, even when it's hard to see it that way right now." Mom's voice was soothing, and I could tell she was trying to be strong for me.

"Yeah, I guess so," I said quietly, thinking about all the good times Ben and I had shared. It was hard to imagine not seeing him every day.

As we approached Ben's apartment, Mom slowed the car. "Remember what I said earlier. Life might pull us in different directions, but if it's meant to be, everything will align eventually. Paths cross for a reason," she said.

I took a deep breath and nodded. "Thanks, Mom."

She smiled softly. "Anytime, sweetheart," she said.

Ben was already waiting outside with his luggage when we pulled up. Seeing him with his carry-on bag outside made my heart skip a beat. Mom hopped out of the car to help him with his luggage. He opened my door and I gave him a tight hug.

"Hey, you," he said, patting my back. Swaying my body. "I'm going to miss you," he said.

"I'm going to miss you too," I replied, my voice catching up. "But we'll see each other soon, right?" I said.

"Absolutely," he said, pulling back and giving me a reassuring smile.

We loaded his bags into the trunk, and he climbed into the backseat. As we drove to the airport, we chatted about all the plans we had for when he came back. It was comforting to talk about the future, even if it felt uncertain.

When we arrived at the airport, Ben hugged Mom.

"Thank you for everything, Heather. Thank you for always making me feel like part of your family," he said.

"You will always be part of our family. Never forget that. Take care and let us know how truly wonderful Norway is," she replied.

"I will," he said.

"This isn't goodbye. It's just a see-you-soon," Mom said.

"I know. We are just a flight away," he said.

"Bye, Ben!" she said.

"Bye," he said.

As we walked into the bustling airport, my heart felt heavier with each step. Ben and I moved through the crowds, finding a quiet corner near the security checkpoint where we could have a moment alone.

"I guess this is it," Ben said softly, setting his carry-on bag down. His eyes were glistening, mirroring the way I felt inside.

"I can't believe you're really leaving," I whispered, my voice trembling. I reached out to hold his hand, the familiar warmth and strength of his grip giving me a momentary comfort.

"I know," he replied, his voice breaking slightly. "I wish I didn't have to go."

"It's just so hard to say goodbye." I said, even though it hurt more than I could put into words.

Ben pulled me into his arms, and I buried my face in his chest, trying to hold back the tears that were threatening to spill over. "It's not goodbye, Madison. It's just a 'see you later.' We'll make it through this, I promise."

I nodded, but the words felt hollow. "I'm going to miss you so much."

"I'm going to miss you too," he said, his voice choked with emotion. "But we'll talk every day, and I'll come back as soon as I can. This isn't the end for us."

Ben cupped my face in his hands, his touch gentle but firm. "No matter where I go or what happens, you'll always be a part of me. Our paths might be different for now, but we'll find our way back to each other. I believe that."

A tear slipped down my cheek, and he wiped it away with his thumb. "I love you, Madison."

"I love you too, Ben," I whispered, feeling the weight of the words. "So much."

The announcement for his flight echoed through the terminal, and Ben sighed, glancing at the gate. "I have to go."

I nodded, unable to speak. He kissed me, a lingering kiss filled with all the things we couldn't say. When he pulled back, he pressed his forehead against mine, closing his eyes.

"Take care of yourself," he murmured. "And remember, this isn't goodbye."

"I'll be waiting for you," I replied, my voice barely a whisper.

He picked up his bag and gave me one last, lingering look, tears in his eyes, before turning towards the security checkpoint. I watched him walk away, each step feeling like a piece of my heart was being torn out.

As he disappeared into the crowd, I stood there, feeling both empty and hopeful. His words echoed in my mind: "We'll find our way back to each other."

I held onto that promise, knowing that no matter how far apart we were, the love we shared would keep us connected.

As I rolled back to the car, the reality of Ben's departure hit me all at once. The airport seemed colder and more overwhelming without him by my side. I tried to keep it together, but the closer I got to the car, the harder it became.

Mom helped me with my chair and I slipped into the passenger seat. She got inside the car, she took one look at me and immediately pulled me into her arms. That was all it took for the dam to break.

I sobbed uncontrollably, my whole body shaking with the force of my emotions. Mom held me tightly, her hand gently stroking my hair. "It's okay, sweetie. Let it out," she whispered, her voice full of empathy and understanding.

"I... I can't believe he's really gone," I managed to choke out between sobs. "It hurts so much, Mom."

"I know, honey. I know," she said softly, her own eyes glistening with unshed tears. "It's never easy saying goodbye to someone you love."

I clung to her, feeling like a child again, seeking comfort in her embrace. "What if... what if things never go back to the way they were?"

Mom sighed, holding me even tighter. "Life changes, Madison. Sometimes it takes us on paths we never expected. But true love finds a way to endure. You and Ben have something special, something strong. Trust in that."

Her words were like a balm, soothing the raw ache in my heart just a little. "I just miss him so much already," I whispered, my voice breaking.

"And that's okay. It's okay to miss him, to feel sad, to cry. It means you care deeply. But remember, this is not the end. It's just a new chapter."

I nodded against her shoulder, trying to find strength in her words. "Thank you, Mom. I don't know what I'd do without you."

She kissed the top of my head, her touch gentle and reassuring. "You don't have to go through this alone, Madison. I'm here for you, always."

I pulled back slightly, looking into her eyes. "I love you, Mom."

"I love you too, sweetheart," she said, wiping away my tears with her thumb. "Now, let's go home. We'll get through this together."

As we drove away from the airport, I kept my eyes on the road ahead, feeling a little more hopeful. The pain was still there, but so was the love and support of my parents. And with that, I knew I could face whatever came next.

# 10 Years Later

# Chapter 20
## Fulfilled Heart

I awoke to the soft chime of my alarm clock, the early morning light filtering through the curtains of my bedroom. Stretching my arms above my head, I felt the familiar sensation of my upper body waking up. With a determined breath, I shifted my attention to the start of my daily routine.

Reaching over to my bedside table, I grabbed my phone and turned off the alarm. Placing it back, I took a moment to glance at the picture frame beside it—a photo of me and my parents from 5 years ago when we went to Hawaii for the first time during the summer. I smiled, feeling a rush of motivation for the day ahead.

Swinging my legs over the side of the bed, I expertly maneuvered myself into my wheelchair, the action fluid and practiced. I rolled into the bathroom, where I brushed my teeth and washed my face, the cool water helping to clear the last remnants of sleep from my mind. I carefully styled my two weeks old short wavy bob hair, tucking a stray lock behind my ear with a smile of satisfaction.

Next, I moved into my closet. I've always loved fashion, and today was no exception. I picked out a crisp white blouse and a pair of tailored black trousers, laying them across my lap as I wheeled myself back to the bed. Getting dressed was a precise process, one I had perfected over the years. My fingers worked nimbly, buttoning the blouse and adjusting my trousers until everything was just right.

I then moved to the kitchen. Placing a coffee pod into the machine, I listened to the comforting hum as it brewed my favorite morning blend. As the aroma of coffee filled the air, I prepared a simple breakfast of avocado toast and fruit, my hands moving swiftly and confidently.

With breakfast done, I took a moment to sip my coffee, enjoying the quiet before the busy day ahead. My eyes wandered to my laptop, which was set up on the dining table. Today's schedule was packed with meetings and deadlines, but I felt ready to tackle it all.

After finishing my coffee, I grabbed my laptop bag, securing it to the back of my wheelchair. I checked my watch—right on time, as always. Taking one last look around my apartment, I ensured everything was in its place before heading out the door.

The elevator ride down to the ground floor was smooth and quick. As I wheeled out into the lobby, I greeted my neighbors with a bright smile and a cheerful "Good morning!" They responded in kind, clearly accustomed to my positive energy.

Outside, the city was waking up. The sound of traffic and the bustle of pedestrians filled the air. I felt a rush of excitement; I loved the energy of the city. Rolling down the familiar parking lot, I made my way to my car, where I would drive a half an hour to my studio.

As I waited for the car to warm up, I took a deep breath, feeling the warmth of the sun on my face. I thought about the challenges and opportunities that awaited me today. Despite any obstacles, I felt ready to face them head-on, confident in my abilities and determined to succeed.

My phone rang.

"Good morning, Emily!" I answered.

"Good morning, sunshine. How was your night?" Emily asked.

"It was good. I slept better than ever. Those melatonin vitamins you recommended put me to sleep like a baby," I said.

"I told you they were good. I usually take them when I need a good night's sleep, especially after Kayleigh has one of those nights where she can't fall asleep easily," she said.

"I can't believe she's three years old already," I said.

"And she's still a bad sleeper. She has always been like that, but it's getting to the point where I'm always exhausted," she said.

"The struggles of being a parent. But she's growing up so fast; I think she'll outgrow this phase in no time," I said.

"I hope so. I feel like I haven't had a full week of good sleep in ages," she said.

"Did you read the email I sent you yesterday?" I asked.

"I did. Are you excited that we have two more kids this month?" she said.

"Our little art class is growing slowly but surely," I said. "I love that we get to do this for a living. I love each new kid that comes to our class. I feel like I have a special bond with them that truly fulfills my heart."

"Speaking of heart, have you talked to Alex?" she asked.

"No, I haven't. It's been two months since I completely cut him out of my life," I said.

"Do you think you'd ever go back to him?" Emily asked.

"Absolutely not. After getting cheated on? Never!" I admitted.

"He was truly a dick for doing that to you," she said.

"I know. Four years of my life went down the drain. Do you know how many things I could've done during those years? I completely gave all of myself to him for nothing, just to get played in the end. He's a loser. I don't want anything to do with him," I said, getting a little heated.

"I'm glad you are finally stepping into your power. Girl, I'm so proud of you. You have been through a lot of shit these past few years and you still manage to push forward. If I had experienced what you did, I would just stay on the ground, letting life pass me by," she said.

"It's called growth. Everything I've experienced has helped me grow as a person. Now I only have time for things and people who bring me joy and who aren't afraid to stay by my side when things get a little rocky," I said.

"Alex who? We don't know him," she said.

"That's right. He's part of my past now," I said. "I'll talk to you when I get there."

"Be careful driving. People are driving like maniacs these days, especially during rush hour," Emily said.

"My anxiety while being in a car has died down ever since I started driving years ago. I feel like now I'm the one in control. I'll be careful, I promise," I said.

"See you soon," she said.

"Bye!" I said.

I backed up my car using the hand controls on my steering wheel and drove straight out of my apartment complex. At the red light I decided to put my sunglasses on, I turned my music up and rolled the windows down to get some fresh air. The cool breeze caressed my face and the wind messed up my hair, but I didn't care. Growing up makes you care less about the things we can't control. My hair this morning was one of those things. North Carolina, the place that has seen me grow, was giving me another beautiful day. That's the only thing that matters.

Stepping inside my art studio, I felt a wave of contentment wash over me. The room was a vibrant explosion of colors, from the bright murals on the walls to the scattered paint splatters on the floor. Sunlight streamed through the large windows, casting a warm glow over everything and making the space feel alive.

I rolled further in, taking a moment to absorb the familiar sights and smells. The scent of acrylic paint and fresh paper mixed with the faint aroma of the flowers I always kept on the windowsill. Each brush, canvas, and paint pot was meticulously arranged, ready for the day's lesson. The shelves were lined with the art supplies I had collected over the years—colored pencils, markers, crayons, and every imaginable shade of paint.

The kids' artwork adorned the walls, their creativity on full display. Each piece was unique, bursting with the unfiltered imagination that only children possess. I felt a swell of pride knowing I had helped guide their little hands and minds in creating these masterpieces.

As I wheeled over to my desk, I couldn't help but smile. This studio was more than just a place to work; it was a sanctuary. It was where I could share my passion for art with the next generation, watching their eyes light up as they discovered new techniques and expressed themselves on canvas.

I started setting up for the class, laying out brushes and palettes, each station a small world of potential waiting to be explored. The anticipation of the kids' arrival buzzed in the air, filling me with a sense of purpose and fulfillment. Seeing their excitement and witnessing their progress brought me more joy than I could ever put into words.

My heart swelled with gratitude. I had created this space from scratch, pouring my soul into every corner. It was a reflection of my journey, my struggles, and my triumphs. This studio was proof that I could overcome any obstacle and achieve my dreams.

As the first little feet patterned through the door, giggles echoing through the room, I felt a deep sense of peace. This was where I belonged. This was where I made a difference. And there was no place I'd rather be.

I gathered all my kids and said goodbye to each of their parents. I assigned each kid their own seat so they don't fight over whose seat is their seat.

"Good morning! How are you guys feeling today?" I said out loud.

"Good morning, Miss Henderson!" most of the kids responded.

"I'm not feeling good today," little Ashley said.

"Ashley, why are you not feeling good today? Do you want to talk about it?" I asked.

"My dog ate half of my Barbie today," she said.

"I'm sorry to hear that, Ash. He probably didn't know how important that Barbie was to you," I said.

"Yeah! He was a bad doggie today, but I forgave him because I love him so much," she said in a cute tone of voice.

"Great attitude. Your Barbie can be replaced, but the love you have for your dog is irreplaceable."

"Miss Henderson, I have a question. What does irreplaceable mean?" Oliver asked.

"It means something that cannot be replaced if lost or damaged," I said.

"She can get a new Barbie at the dollar store. My mom bought one for my sister for five dollars," Max said.

"Did you hear that, Ash? Material things can be replaced," I said.

"It's okay. I have other ones that I can play with," she said.

"Can you guys help me welcome Chelsea and Theo? They are going to be joining us for our art adventures," I said.

"Hi Chelsea and Theo!" they all said.

"Miss Henderson, why are you sitting in a wheelchair?" Theo asked.

"When I was younger, I had a big car accident that changed some things for me. Now, I can't use my legs to walk. But guess what? This cool wheelchair is like my super legs! It helps me zoom around and do everything I want to do, just like you use your legs. It's my special way to move and have fun!" I said.

"I have a bicycle that has wheels like your chair," Theo said.

"They do look very similar to the wheels on a bicycle. Good observation! See, we all have something in common, no matter how different we may be," I said.

Suddenly, I remembered how that question used to bother me so much when I had recently become paralyzed. Now, I'm not embarrassed to show the world how unique I am. I've come so far, and I'm proud of myself for that. I embrace who I truly am instead of trying to hide in my shell. My disability no longer defines who I am. I am so much more than just the woman in a wheelchair.

"Are you guys ready to have fun?" I said.

"Yeah!" they all replied.

The kids had been painting for the last hour, and their creativity was unleashed in vibrant splashes of reds, blues, and yellows. I walked around the room, my heart swelling with pride as I watched their little hands maneuver brushes with the kind of reckless abandon only children possess. The smell of paint and the gentle hum of chatter filled the air, creating a symphony of joy that made my heart sing.

"Look, Miss Henderson!" Mia, a bubbly seven-year-old, called out to me, her face smeared with green paint. "I made a rainbow unicorn!"

I leaned in to examine her masterpiece, a riot of colors that seemed to leap off the page. "It's beautiful, Mia! I love how you mixed the colors. It looks like magic!"

Her eyes lit up, and she beamed at me, her smile as bright as the sun. I moved on, pausing at each table to offer words of encouragement and admiration. Each painting was a unique window into their imaginations, an opened door to their boundless creativity.

At the back of the room, Tommy was deep in concentration, his tongue poking out as he carefully added details to his dragon. I leaned beside him, marveling at the intricate scales and fiery breath. "That's an amazing dragon, Tommy. You have such a talent for details."

He looked up at me, his eyes wide with surprise. "You really think so, Miss Henderson?"

"Absolutely. Keep it up, you're doing great."

As I looked back up, I caught sight of Emily standing by the supply cabinet, her eyes twinkling as she watched the scene unfold. Her presence was a comforting anchor, a reminder of why we started this journey together. Emily had been my rock, my partner in this beautiful chaos, and seeing her now, amidst the laughter and creativity, filled me with a profound sense of gratitude.

I made my way over to her, dodging a few enthusiastic brush-wielders along the way. When I reached her, I couldn't help but smile. "Can you believe this is our life?" I asked, my voice soft with wonder.

Emily's gaze met mine, and she nodded, a slow, contented smile spreading across her face. "It's everything we dreamed of, isn't it?"

I looked back at the room, at the kids who were so full of life and potential, and then back at Emily. "Yes, it is. And so much more."

We shared a moment of quiet understanding, standing side by side as the joyful noise of the classroom wrapped around us. This was the life we had chosen, a life filled with color, creativity, and the pure, unfiltered happiness of children discovering their own artistic voices. And in that moment, I knew, without a doubt, that it was the best decision we had ever made.

# Chapter 21
## Letting Go of the Idea of Forever

It's Dylan's birthday today. It's hard to wrap my mind around the fact that it has been ten years since he passed away. The years have flown by with a swiftness that feels almost cruel, blurring the edges of memories I wish I could hold onto forever. It seems like only yesterday we were celebrating his laughter and his life together.

This morning, I decided to honor his memory in a small but meaningful way. I made my way to the nearest dollar store, a humble place filled with trinkets and treasures. I wandered the aisles, my eyes scanning the colorful array of party supplies until I found them—balloons emblazoned with cheerful "Happy Birthday" messages. They were bright and festive, a stark contrast to the somber occasion, but somehow it felt right. Dylan always loved a good celebration, and I wanted to bring that joy to his resting place.

Next, I drove to Trader Joe's. As soon as I stepped inside, the floral section caught my eye, a vibrant display of seasonal blooms. The air was filled with their fresh, earthy scent, and for a moment, I just stood there, letting the fragrances wash over me. I knew immediately what I wanted. Sunflowers. Their bold, golden faces seemed to capture the essence of summer, and they were always Dylan's favorite.

I selected a bouquet, the flowers' petals warm and bright against my skin. They felt alive, brimming with a warmth that mirrored the sunny day outside. Holding them close, I could almost feel Dylan's presence, as if he was smiling down at me, appreciating the small gesture of love and remembrance.

With the balloons and flowers in tow, I left the store, the weight of time pressing down on me. A decade gone, yet his memory remained as vivid as ever. I hoped that wherever he was, he could see the care and thought I put into celebrating his special day, even in his absence.

I arrived at the cemetery, parked my car, and stepped out, the gravel crunching beneath my wheels. Maneuvering through the gravel was challenging, but I pushed through as I always do. The sky is a brilliant blue, with not a cloud in sight, and the sun casts a golden glow over everything. It's the kind of day that begs for picnics and laughter, not for cemetery visits. But here I am, taking slow, deliberate pushes toward where my best friend rests.

As I made my way through the cemetery, the breeze ruffled the leaves of the towering oak trees lining the pathway. The cemetery is quiet, save for the distant hum of the city that never quite fades away. Life is always in a rush out there, but here, time seems to stand still.

I finally found his grave, nestled among the rows of stones that mark the resting places of so many others. Each tombstone reminded me not to worry about the future. All these people were living at some point in their life's journey and now they had become just a mere memory of their once presence.

I felt at peace here. I took my time walking along the concrete pathway. Why rush? My mind kept reminding me. "We all end up here in the end anyway," my subconscious mused. A few balloons were already placed around his tombstone, their colors vibrant against the gray granite. Someone else had remembered, too. The sight of those balloons brought a lump to my throat.

I stood there in the quiet, the wind gently blowing a few strands of my hair across my face. The cemetery was serene, almost peaceful, but I was overwhelmed by the weight of my emotions. I could feel the familiar sting of tears welling up in my eyes. No matter how many years pass, coming here always stirs the same deep sadness within me. I can't help but wonder how different life would be if he were still here, how his presence would have shaped my world.

Lost in my thoughts, I reached into my pocket and pulled out a folded piece of paper. It was a letter I had written the night before, filled with all the things I wished I could say to him. "I wrote you a letter." I said, while I unfolded the paper. "I mean, I could use the notes app on my phone, but there's nothing like writing your feelings out with a pen and paper as if we were in the eighteen hundreds. Someone special in my life wrote me a letter like this once and I thought you would love it as much as I did back then." I took a deep breath and began to read it aloud, my voice trembling slightly. There was no one around to hear me anyway, just the rustling leaves and the distant chirping of birds.

"Dear Dylan,

It's hard to find the right words, I don't know if they will ever reach you. Yet, I feel the need to speak to you, to share the thoughts and feelings that have settled in my heart since you left. I miss you so much. There's not a single day that I don't think about you. I miss your voice, our silly conversations, your laughter, your hugs and your companionship. Losing you has taught me a profound lesson about letting go of the idea of forever.

When you were here, it was easy to believe in forever. Our friendship felt timeless, as if it would always be a constant in my life. We made plans, dreamed big, and laughed about growing old together. But your sudden departure shattered that illusion and forced me to confront the fragile nature of life and the impermanence of everything we hold dear.

In the days and months since you've been gone, I've struggled to accept that forever is not something we can count on. At first, it was a painful realization. The idea that something as wonderful as our friendship could be so abruptly cut short felt unfair and deeply saddening.

But over time, I've come to understand that while forever may be an illusion, the moments we shared were real and incredibly precious.

I've learned to cherish the present and appreciate the people in my life more deeply. Your absence has taught me that every moment is a gift, and that we should hold our loved ones close and make the most of the time we have with them. The memories we created together, though finite, are filled with so much joy and meaning. They are a testament to the beauty of the time we spent together.

Letting go of the idea of forever has also taught me about resilience and finding strength in vulnerability. It's okay to grieve, to feel the weight of loss, and to miss you every day. But it's also important to honor your memory by living fully and embracing the present with an open heart.

Sometimes, we have to let go of the people we love, even though it's one of the hardest things to do. Letting go doesn't mean forgetting or loving them any less; it means accepting that our paths have diverged, and finding peace in the fact that we were fortunate enough to share part of our journey with them. In letting go, we honor the love we shared and allow ourselves to move forward, carrying their memory as a source of strength and inspiration.

Dylan, I carry you with me in all that I do. Your friendship has shaped who I am, and the lessons I've learned from losing you continue to guide me. I'm grateful for every moment we shared, and I promise to live in a way that honors the love and laughter we experienced together.

Thank you for everything, my dear friend. You may not be here physically, but your memory lives on in my heart, reminding me to treasure each day and every connection I make.

Your eternal friend,

Madison"

The wind picked up, and I felt a chill despite the warmth of the summer day. The reality of his absence hit me all over again, a heavy, familiar ache. I finished reading the letter, my voice barely a whisper by the end. I folded the paper and tucked it back into my pocket, feeling a small sense of relief for having shared my thoughts, even if only with the wind and the stones.

A butterfly flitted past, catching the sunlight on its beautiful pattern wings, and I smiled through my tears.

I took a single sunflower and placed it in front of his tombstone.

Happy Birthday, Dylan! I hope you're dancing and being the beautiful light that you are wherever you are. Please give my mom a hug for me.

# Chapter 22

# Time Will Tell

"Hi Emily! How are you doing?" I answered my phone.

"I already feel exhausted, and it's only eleven in the morning. I don't know why I decided to use my free time to clean this house that never looks clean, no matter how hard I try. Taking two hours of my Saturday to tidy up feels like a never-ending challenge. Brandon took Kayleigh to the park so she could burn off some energy, and I could try to make this place a little more presentable," Emily said.

"I asked you if you wanted to go to Barnes & Noble today, but you rejected my offer. You decided to play Cinderella instead," I said.

"You should come babysit Kayleigh more often so I can live your life for a day or two. I'm jealous," she said.

"Whenever you want. I told you I love spending time with her," I said.

"What are you picking up at Barnes? You have a massive TBR list of books you haven't even touched," she said.

"It's not that bad. I have like eight books waiting for me on my bookshelf," I confessed.

"Exactly my point. What are you getting this time?" Emily asked.

"I'm just going to browse the romance aisle. I'm on the hunt for an enemies-to-lovers trope novel today," I said.

"Spice level?" she asked.

"A one and a half. I don't like that kinky stuff. It's not my thing. I'm not up for that 'I can feel him inside me, pressing his hips against my pelvis while he furiously grabs my left breast and plays with my nipple.' At least not today," I said.

"You mean literary soft porn?" Emily said.

"That should be a section at the bookstore. It ruins the romance for me all the time. I would love to find a fluffy, comforting, tear-jerking romance like 'The Notebook' or something similar," I said.

"But sex is part of a relationship," she said.

"But you don't go telling people what you did in bed with your significant other," I said.

"I think you're missing the point. That's what makes it intimate," she said.

"You're right. Still not my thing, though," I said.

"For how long are you going to be at Barnes?" she asked.

"Like an hour and a half-ish. Why?" I said.

"Just asking. Let me know when you get there. Are you going to the same one you always go to?" she asked.

"Yes. What's up with all these random questions? Are you coming to Barnes with me?" I said.

"No. I wish," she said.

"Do you have a surprise for me?" I asked.

"Maybe," she said.

"Should I be worried?" I asked.

"No, I don't think so," she replied.

"Can you tell me now? You know I hate surprises," I said.

"That would ruin the surprise," she said.

"Emily!" I said.

"It's nothing you're going to hate," she said.

"Are you finally giving me my birthday gift that you told me you were going to get me like six months ago?" I said.

"I still have to work on that," she said.

"Okay, fine. I'm giving up. Whatever it is, I hope it's something that brings me joy. I need more of that," I said.

"Oh, you're going to love it," she said.

"Do you want me to get you something while I'm there?" I asked.

"Can you check if they have a signed copy of Megan Smith's new book?" she said.

"I love her books. The one where the main character falls in love with her bodyguard—I forgot the name of it. Anyway, I've heard so many good things about it. I could do that for you," I said.

"The title is Close Encounter. If you see one, grab it for me. I'll Venmo you the money," she said.

"Anything else?" I asked.

"I don't think so. Let me get back to my cleaning duties. I want to finish at least our main bathroom today. Text me when you get there," she said.

"Are you sure you're not going to tell me anything about the surprise?" I asked.

"Nope. Love you, talk to you later," she said.

"Did she just hang up on me?" I said out loud, alone in my car. "I really hope she didn't set me up on a blind date. I'm not in the mood to deal with men today," I said to myself while checking my purse to make sure I had my wallet.

Walking into Barnes & Noble for my monthly trip felt like stepping into a familiar embrace. The soft hum of classical music played over the speakers, mingling with the quiet murmur of other people and the comforting rustle of pages being turned. The scent of freshly brewed coffee from the café mixed with the earthy aroma of paper and ink, a scent that had always brought me an inexplicable sense of peace.

Barnes & Noble has always been more than just a bookstore to me. It was a haven, a place where I could find pieces of myself in the stories of others. Whether I needed an escape, a companion, or simply a moment of peace, I knew I could find it here, surrounded by the words and worlds that had shaped my life.

As I wandered through the aisles, my fingers traced the spines of countless books, each one a potential journey waiting to be taken. Books have been my constant companions through every high and low in life. When I was a child, stories of fantastical adventures and brave heroes had been my escape from the ordinary. During the tumultuous teenage years, I found solace in pages filled with angst and heartache, knowing that others had felt as I did and had made it through to the other side.

Even now, as an adult, books remained my sanctuary. In moments of joy, I would devour light-hearted romances and whimsical fantasies, my laughter mingling with the words on the page. During the darkest times, when life felt too heavy to bear, I found comfort in the familiar weight of a novel in my hands, the promise of another world where anything was possible. I remembered the nights spent curled up in bed, a cup of hot cocoa by my side, finding refuge in the words of authors who seemed to understand the deepest parts of my soul.

Today, I was on the hunt for something new, something that would resonate with my current state of mind. I stopped in front of a display of new releases, my eyes scanning the covers, searching for one that spoke to me. A particular book caught my eye—a deep blue cover with an intricate gold design. I picked it up, feeling the smoothness of the dust jacket under my fingers, and read the blurb on the back.

"Will she end up with Jake Monroe, the town's swoon-worthy new fireman with abs sculpted by the gods and a smile that could melt even the coldest of hearts." I whispered.

"Excuse me!" I heard a man say, the voice coming from behind me.

"Oh no. You definitely don't want to read that," I said, embarrassed of my book choice without seeing who he was.

"That's okay, I'm not into fictional love stories. Just the real ones," he said.

"You're in the wrong book section then!" I said, turning around.

"Ben?" I said, surprised.

"Hi Madison!" he said.

My immediate reaction was to hug him, and I did so without a second thought. As I pulled him into my arms, a rush of emotions overwhelmed me. The warmth of his body against mine was both familiar and foreign, a bittersweet reminder of what I'd missed. My heart pounded in my chest, a mixture of joy, relief, and lingering regret. I could feel his heartbeat too, syncing with mine, as if no time had passed at all. The scent of his hair, the softness of his touch, it all brought back a flood of memories. I held him tighter, afraid to let go, savoring the comfort and peace that came from being close to him again. All around me faded away, and all that mattered was that he was here, with me.

"It feels like I haven't seen you in forever," I said.

"About seven years," he replied.

"What are you doing here in the States?" I asked.

"I moved back to North Carolina. I'm going to finish the last two years of my doctorate here in the US," he said.

"That's great to hear. Wow, pretty soon you'll be a real doctor," I said.

"That's right. It's crazy how fast time flies," he said.

"It does. I'm still mad at you, though," I said.

"Why?" he asked.

"You really broke my heart," I said.

"Let me invite you over for some coffee. We can sit and have a chat. If you want to?" he asked.

"Yeah, sure. I was going to pick up an iced vanilla latte on my way out, so perfect timing," I said.

"You look pretty as always. I like your short hair," he said.

"Thank you! I was craving change, so I chopped it all off. It gave me the fresh start I wanted," I said.

"How have you been since the passing of your mom?" he asked.

"It's been difficult, I'm not going to lie. Some days are better than others, but I try to stay positive as much as I can. She definitely wouldn't want me to live a sad life. I make sure to make most of my days worth living," I said.

"Tell me about you. I like your outfit, by the way. You look older, in a good way," I said.

"Because I'm thirty-four now, and thank you. I try to look more professional nowadays. I try way too hard to look my age. I miss wearing my sweatshirts and shorts all the time. But yeah, I've been working hard to accomplish my goal of becoming a psychologist. My life has been focused on my studies for the past decade," he said.

"Hi! What can I get for you guys today?" the coffee shop employee said.

"Can I please get a small cold brew and an iced vanilla latte?" he said. "What size do you want?"

"A small," I said.

"And a small iced vanilla latte, please. That would be all," he said.

"Alright, that is going to be a total of ten dollars and eighty-five cents," the employee said.

"Let me pay for my coffee," I said.

"Don't worry about it. I got you," he said.

We grabbed our coffees. I tasted mine through the straw and it was perfect. We sat in a corner of the coffee shop where it was more secluded from other people. I sat across Ben looking directly into his eyes. Time has passed, but I still have strong feelings for him. Seeing him again woke up the same feelings that I had for him years ago.

"No sugar or anything in that cold brew," I said.

"I try my best to consume the least amount of sugar possible. Can't be talking about health and not practicing what I preach," he said.

"Ready for our therapy session then?" I asked, smiling.

He took a sip of his cold brew. "Listening," he said.

"I just want to know why you stopped talking to me and ended up cutting all sorts of communication with me?" I asked.

"I didn't want to keep you waiting for me. I knew my career was going to take all my time. I didn't want you to stay on the sidelines for me. To me, it was not fair for you," he said.

"And how did you know how I truly felt? We can't assume what other people think. I told you I was willing to stay by your side no matter what. I knew how demanding your career was going to be, and I was okay with the idea of fully supporting you even if you didn't have much time to juggle everything. You just gave up on us," I said.

"I just wanted you to be happy," he said.

"But you made me happy. I was focusing on trying to find myself, whether it was with you by my side or not. It wasn't like I was fully clinging to you and not having my own self-identity. I wanted us to grow together as individuals," I said.

"I guess I also didn't want you to leave everything behind for me, especially your family. I knew how important they were in your life. I didn't want to take that from you by moving to Norway with me," he said.

"We could've made it work. We would have figured it out like we always did," I said.

"I'm sorry. I truly am. Just know that all my intentions came from a place of love. I thought letting you go was the best way to ensure you had the freedom to find your own path and happiness," he said.

"But my happiness was intertwined with yours. I was ready to support you, to be patient, and to find joy in the moments we could share. You underestimated my love and commitment," I said.

"I see that now, and I'm so sorry for not realizing it sooner. I was trying to protect you, but in doing so, I hurt you and pushed you away," he said.

"You really did. And it hurt more because I never stopped loving you," I admitted.

"I have never stopped loving you too. I've thought of you every day for the past ten years," he said.

I looked away, processing his words.

Benson was staring at me, eyes searching, a mix of confusion and something else I couldn't quite place.

"Madison," he finally said, his voice steady but his eyes betraying his struggle. "Why did you start dating Alex?"

I sighed, placing my coffee gently on the table. This was a conversation I'd been dreading, but I knew it had to happen sooner or later. Benson deserved an explanation, even if I wasn't sure he'd understand.

"Benson," I began, choosing my words carefully, "it wasn't something I planned. It just... happened."

His brow furrowed, and he leaned back in his chair, crossing his arms over his chest. "Just happened? Madison, you know how I feel about Alex. He's... not the kind of guy I expected you to go for."

I nodded, feeling the weight of his disappointment. "I know. But you have to understand, it's not about what you expected or even what I expected. It's about how I felt when I was with him."

"And how is that?" Benson's tone was sharp, almost accusatory, but I knew it stemmed from hurt, not anger.

"Different," I admitted. "He made me feel different, Benson. He saw a side of me that I didn't even know existed. It was exciting and terrifying all at once."

Benson's expression softened slightly, but the confusion remained. "But Madison, he's so... unpredictable. He's the complete opposite of everything you've always wanted."

I looked down at my coffee, swirling it absentmindedly. "Maybe that's why it felt right. I've spent so much of my life trying to fit into this mold of what I thought I wanted, what everyone thought I should want. But with Alex, it was like I can just... be."

He sighed, and for a moment, I saw a flash of something in his eyes—pain, maybe even jealousy. "I just didn't see it coming. You and Alex... it's so out of the blue."

"I know." I said softly.

Benson took a long sip of his coffee, as if buying time to process what I'd said. "I just want you to be happy, Madison."

"I appreciate that. More than you know. But I need to figure this out for myself. At least now I understand that your intentions were pure and came from a place of love. It makes it a bit easier to forgive you," I said.

"I regret the pain I caused, and I wish I could turn back time and make different choices. I hope you can find it in your heart to forgive me," he said.

"I already did. I care about you a lot. I will always have a special place in my heart for you. It would take a lot for me to ever hate you. I never had a wrong idea about you," I said.

"Is it too late to say that I still love you?" he asked.

"Ben, I would never erase all we had. Time will tell," I said.

"Time will tell," he said, looking into my eyes.

A serene silence settled between us. Silence with someone you love is a different kind of quiet. It's a stillness that wraps around you, warm and comforting, like a soft blanket on a chilly evening. With Benson, our silences were never empty or awkward. They were filled with an unspoken understanding, a shared history that didn't need words to be acknowledged.

Silence with Benson was filled with trust, love, and the unshakeable certainty that we were meant to be together. It was a reminder that the strongest connections aren't always about what is said, but about what is felt, deeply and unmistakably, in the quiet moments shared between two hearts.

"Let me walk you to your car before I go," he said.

"Can't wait to show you how I drive now," I said.

"So that means you can pick me up from my place?" he asked.

"Now you can be my passenger princess," I said, smiling.

"I'm down with that," he said.

We both laughed. I'm glad that nothing has changed.

# Chapter 23
## Second Chances

"I'm arriving at your apartment complex. Where do I park?" I said, inside my car with the phone on speaker.

"Park on the right side of the building. There are usually some parking spots next to the sidewalk," Benson said. "Do you see them?"

"The ones close to the dumpster?" I asked.

"Yeah, those ones. Is there a parking spot available?" Ben said.

"I see two of them," I said.

"Great! I'll be down in a minute," he said, hanging up our call.

I've gotten really good at parallel parking, sometimes even impressing myself. Not like when I hit every curb learning how to drive with hand controls. It was a struggle getting back behind the wheel at first. I was anxious and fearful of getting into an accident. But look at me now, driving by myself. Another simple thing that makes me proud these days.

I heard a knock on the passenger-side window. I opened the door for Ben, and the smell of his cologne filled the car.

"Hey!" he said, giving me a hug.

"Hi! You smell nice," I said.

"I recently got a new perfume. Do you like it?" he asked.

"It smells like a smoky wood. It's really good," I said.

"It's the Le Labo Santal 33," he said.

"Oh, boujee! You paid two hundred dollars for a bottle of perfume?" I said.

"Yes, I did! And I have zero regrets," he said.

"It does smell like a two-hundred-dollar perfume, though," I said.

"I put it on today so every time we hug, you can smell the scent of regret," he joked.

I laughed. "That's not going to work. Regret of what?" I said, putting my car in reverse.

"Of still not giving me a second chance," he said.

"I already did. We are hanging out like the good old days," I said.

"That's true! How have you been? How's your art studio going?" he asked.

"It's been great. I love every second of it. I love that I get to share my passion with future generations and inspire them to pursue what they love. My kids are amazing. I learn from them every single day. We are looking forward to growing slowly," I said.

"Nice! What a dream it has been seeing you flourish into this entrepreneur phase, especially when a few years ago you were so confused about what you really wanted to do in life," he said.

"I found my path in life by just doing what I love. That's it. That's how you find yourself. What's new with you?" I said.

"Did I tell you that I started talking to my parents again?" he said.

"You did? That makes me so happy to hear," I said, surprised.

"I forgave them. Who was I to judge them? Especially now that I'm getting older, I understand that none of us have life figured out. They are also experiencing life for the first time. There's no manual for life. We are all doing the best we can with what we've got. I didn't want to be mad at them for the rest of my life," he said.

"I'm glad you did. Life is too short to hold grudges. I can't wait to meet them one day. I want to get to know the people who brought you into this world. I'm so genuinely happy for you," I said.

"Thank you," he said. "Isn't it crazy how time changes everything?"

"It really does," I said, stopping at a red light.

"Can I ask you why you and Alex split up?" he asked.

"He cheated on me," I admitted.

"What a jerk," he said.

"You were right in the first place. I should have listened to your instincts that day at the gallery event. When we first started dating, he was this charming, sometimes too extroverted person. Always being a little too nice with everyone around him. He always wanted to meet new people and be at every social event he could. It's like he never had deep connections with a few people; he wanted to meet half the population. And just like that, he replaced me. I think he fell into the trap of having too many options," I said.

"So he basically passed up the opportunity of being with someone like you. Interesting," he said.

"He did! And sadly, he destroyed my confidence a bit too. I started to look down on myself for having a disability. I wrongly thought that could be why he did something like that, but I'm grateful I got out of that mindset and realized he was the one who did everything wrong. But here I am, stronger than ever," I said.

"I'm sorry you experienced all of that," he said.

"It's not how I pictured my life to be, but here we are," I said.

"Here we are," he repeated. "Life can take some unexpected turns."

"It sure does," I said.

"Does your dad need anything for the barbecue?" he said.

"No. He just said to make sure to invite you over. I haven't seen him that excited to see someone in a long time," I said.

"Really?" Ben said.

"When are you going to invite Ben over to hang out? He repeated that to me for the longest time. So he's excited to see you," I said.

"That's awesome. I can't wait to see him too. How has he handled your mom's passing?" he asked.

"Ben, you're going to make me cry," I said.

"I'm sorry. I didn't mean to," he said.

"It's been tough seeing him alone. It's like he started a new chapter in his life. He spends a lot of time alone. I try to call him every single day. Thankfully, he focuses his time on woodworking projects around the house. It's been tough not having Mom here anymore. We miss everything about her. I miss those simple moments with her, like our conversations at the dinner table or going out with her to run errands. Those simple moments are the ones that I miss the most. The little insignificant moments that you don't appreciate until you lose someone," I said.

"You are not alone. You know you can count on me for anything you need. If you or your dad need someone to talk to, just let me know. Now that I'm more knowledgeable in psychology, I can help you navigate your process of grief," he said.

"For free?" I joked.

"No, for five hundred dollars an hour," he said, smiling. "No, I'm serious."

"Thank you! I appreciate that," I said.

"You're welcome," he said.

Going back to my parents' home feels very nostalgic. I miss those days when I used to sit on the front porch to read a good book and occasionally stare at the trees and the beautiful blue sky.

"Dad!" I called while knocking on the door.

The door swung open.

"Sweetie, you're home!" Dad said, giving me a hug.

I had Benson hide next to the garage door to surprise my dad.

"Look who finally came to visit you," I said, looking at Ben and Dad. I wanted to cherish this moment.

"Benson!" Dad said.

"James! How's it going? I haven't seen you in ages," Ben said.

"I know. It's been a few years," Dad said.

Ben extended his hand to greet my dad, who shook it and then gave him a hug.

"I'm so happy to see you. Look at you! You've grown up so much," Dad said.

"I've grown older. Now my knees crack every time I get up from the floor," Ben said.

"Wait till you turn my age. Come inside; I marinated some chicken for you guys so we can have a nice barbecue. Do you want something to drink?" Dad asked.

"Water would be fine for me, Dad," I said.

"And Ben, what would you like? I have beer, Coke Zero, iced tea, or water," Dad said.

"Water is fine, thank you," Ben said.

The familiar scent of Dad's coffee hit me first, mingling with the faint mustiness that had settled in the corners of rooms rarely used. It was the same house, yet everything felt different. The absence of Mom's laughter, her soft humming as she moved about the kitchen, left an eerie silence that seemed to echo off the walls.

The living room was just as she left it, with her favorite quilt folded neatly on the arm of the couch and the photos of our family vacations still lining the mantel. I could almost hear her voice telling me to help her water the patio plants. But that voice, so warm and comforting, was now just a memory.

I moved slowly, each push feeling heavier than the last. The dining table was set for one instead of three, only one placemat placed on the table, the spot where he always sat, a painful reminder that our family was incomplete. Dad's chair, the one at the head of the table, looked more worn than I remembered, the cushion bearing the weight of long, lonely evenings.

I found myself in the entryway of the kitchen, staring at the spot where Mom used to stand, cooking up meals that filled the house with mouth-watering aromas. The kitchen felt cold now, despite the sunlight streaming through the window. Her apron still hung on the hook by the door, a ghost of her presence that tugged painfully at my heart.

It had been a year, but the wound still felt fresh, as if she had just walked out the door and never returned. The house, once filled with her vibrant energy, now felt like a shell, an empty echo of what it used to be.

"Here you go, sweetie, and a water bottle for you, sir," Dad said. "Maddie told me that you are close to getting your PhD."

"I am. Two more years of studying, and I can finally call myself a psychologist," Ben said.

"That's awesome. Do you remember how you told me your future plans at the dinner table?" Dad said.

"Just like yesterday," Ben said.

"And here we are, ten years later. I'm so proud of you!" Dad said.

"Thank you! I appreciate that," Ben said.

"You really did prove me wrong. I was like, 'Do you even have a future plan?' Remember when I questioned your intentions with Madison?" Dad said.

"I do remember," Ben said.

"And what about you two?" Dad asked.

"Dad," I said, knowing where this conversation was going.

"Have you thought about getting back together?" Dad asked.

"Dad!" I said, trying my best to stop him from talking more about the topic.

"What? You're done with that clown who disrespected you, and honestly, I think in my humble opinion, you both are destined to be together. You make a great couple," Dad said.

"We do make a great couple. I've let her know how I truly feel, but Madison is thinking about it too much," Ben said.

"Maddie! Why is that?" Dad said, looking at me like he was disappointed.

"What is this, couples therapy?" I said.

"I just said I really needed time to think about it," I admitted.

"Time goes by so quickly. If you really love each other, I think you should give it a chance. Long distance and miscommunication broke your relationship. You're both more mature now. I really think you can work this through," Dad said.

"I know, right? I'm willing to accept however she wants to pursue our relationship. If she wants to stay friends, I'll accept that. We've been through so much together that at this point, I just want her to do whatever is best for her. But I'm not going anywhere this time around. I want her in my life forever, as a friend or a future wife," Ben said.

"You heard that, Maddie! As a future wife," Dad said, enjoying the conversation to the fullest. His reactions were kind of funny.

"Dad, you're not helping. Didn't we come here to have a nice summer barbecue? Why are you putting me on the spot?" I said, sweating a little.

"I'm not. You have history together. I'm just wondering why you're not back together yet. When I was dating your mom, I couldn't picture my life without her. Now that I see you together again, I feel the same energy I experienced with her. I'm pretty sure your mom would think the same," Dad said.

I took a sip from my water bottle. I looked at Ben, and he made a face that looked like he was onto something. He stayed really quiet during this out-of-the-blue intervention. Dad did earn some brownie points from him.

The sun was just beginning to dip below the horizon, casting a warm, golden light over the backyard as Dad and Benson fired up the grill. The scent of charcoal mingled with the sweet, smoky aroma of chicken sizzling on the grates, and my mouth watered in anticipation.

I sat at the picnic table, watching Benson expertly turn the corn on the cob, its kernels turning a perfect shade of golden brown. He glanced over at me and flashed a playful grin. "Get ready for the best barbecue chicken you've ever had, Madison," he teased.

Dad chuckled, flipping a piece of chicken with a satisfying sizzle. "He's not wrong, you know. Benson's got a real talent for this."

The three of us chatted and laughed, the conversation flowing as easily as the cool breeze that rustled the leaves of the trees shading our little gathering. Benson recounted a funny story from work, and Dad shared a memory from one of our past family barbecues, his eyes twinkling with nostalgia.

When the food was ready, Benson carefully placed the perfectly grilled chicken and corn on the table. I eagerly picked up a piece of chicken, the crispy skin giving way to tender, juicy meat beneath. The first bite was heaven—smoky, savory, with just the right hint of spice. The corn was equally delicious, buttery and sweet, with a satisfying crunch.

"Wow, Dad," I said between bites, "this is amazing. Seriously, you should consider opening a restaurant."

He laughed, his eyes crinkling at the corners. "Only if you promise to be my first customer."

I smiled, feeling a warmth spread through me that had nothing to do with the summer evening. As the sun dipped lower, casting long shadows across the yard, I couldn't help but picture more evenings like this—Benson and me, surrounded by family, sharing meals and laughter, creating a lifetime of memories.

Dad raised his glass of iced tea in a toast. "To good food and even better company."

We clink our glasses together, the sound a small, perfect moment in the larger tapestry of the evening. I caught Benson's eye over the rim of my glass, and in that brief, silent exchange, I felt a promise of a future filled with love, laughter, and countless barbecues just like this one.

As we got inside the house, I took a peek into my parents' bedroom. I could see that Dad still had not gotten rid of Mom's stuff. Her closet was still full of clothes.

"Hey, Dad! Whenever you feel ready to go through Mom's clothes, call me so I can help you out. There are a lot of things here that we can donate," I said.

"I haven't done it because it feels like I'm getting rid of her, of who she was," Dad said.

I gave him a hug.

"She will always be with us. We're never going to forget about her. That's why I want to help you organize the closet and donate her things so we can move on. She wouldn't want us to stop living. I want to see you go back to the person you were before Mom passed away," I said.

"That's going to take me a while," he confessed.

"We'll get through it together," I said as we both stood there looking at the closet.

"You can also turn my old bedroom into a guest room so I can stay with you whenever I visit. You don't have to keep my room the way it is. It's time to start a new chapter. That could be your new project. You can even turn it into a home office," I suggested.

"That would be nice. My own space where I can have my desktop and everything," Dad said.

"Absolutely! A space to accommodate your needs," I said.

"You're right. Thank you for coming over. I enjoyed spending time with both of you. Ben, please don't disappear for the next ten years," Dad said.

"Oh, I won't, I promise. I think I'm going to stay in North Carolina for the long run. I promise I'll come visit you more often," Ben said.

"Of course, whenever you want. We are like family," Dad said.

"Dad, thank you for the leftovers. That barbecue chicken was phenomenal," I said, folding the edges of the tin foil wrapped around a ceramic plate.

"You have to come over one day so I can show you the recipe," Dad said.

"I have to. See you soon," I said, giving him the tightest hug. I learned to hug the people I love.

Life taught me that tomorrow is not guaranteed.
"I'll come over this week to start that closet
project."

"Bye, Dad!" I said.

"James, see you soon!" Ben said, putting a
gentle hand on my dad's back.

"Drive safely," Dad said in a serious tone.

"I will!" I reassured him.

## Chapter 24
## True Love

Four Months Later

I adjusted my sign for the fifth time, ensuring the letters were perfectly aligned. "Run, Benson, Run!" it read in bright, bold colors. Below that, "I Love You!" was written in smaller, but equally vibrant letters. I couldn't help but smile every time I looked at it. Benson had been training for this half marathon for months, and today was finally the big day.

The finish line area was buzzing with excitement. Spectators cheered as runners began crossing, each one looking exhausted but elated. I scanned the crowd, my eyes darting from one sweaty face to another, searching for Benson. The sun was high now, casting a warm glow over everything. Despite the heat, a breeze provided a bit of relief, rustling through the trees and lifting my spirits.

I glanced down at my legs, a reminder of my own journey. Becoming a paraplegic had been a challenge I never expected to face, but it had brought Benson and me closer together. His determination to support me through everything made me love him even more. And now, here I was, ready to support him as he accomplished something incredible.

The announcer's voice boomed over the loudspeakers, calling out the names of runners as they crossed the finish line. I watched as one after another passed by, each one pushing through the last few yards with every ounce of strength they had left.

Then, I saw him. Benson's familiar stride, a mix of fatigue and resolve, emerged from the pack. His face was a blend of focus and exhaustion, but when our eyes met, a spark of recognition and joy lit up his expression. I held up my sign high, waving it back and forth, hoping he could see it clearly. "Run, Benson, Run! I Love You!"

He pushed through the final steps, crossing the finish line with a triumphant yell. I could see the mixture of relief and pride wash over him as he slowed to a stop, hands on his knees, breathing heavily. I wheeled myself forward, eager to be the first to congratulate him.

"Benson!" I called out, my voice almost lost in the sea of cheering and clapping.

He looked up, spotted me, and a wide grin spread across his face. He jogged over, dropping to his knees in front of me. His sweat-drenched face was flushed, but his eyes sparkled with happiness.

"You did it!" I said, my voice full of admiration. "You were amazing!"

Benson laughed, reaching out to take my hand. "I couldn't have done it without you," he replied, his voice hoarse but filled with affection. "That sign is perfect, Madison. Thank you."

I squeezed his hand, feeling a rush of love and pride. "I'm so proud of you, Benson. You're incredible."

He leaned in, pressing a soft kiss to my forehead. "No, Madison. We're incredible."

We got home at our apartment where we have been living together for the past month and a half. I sometimes can't believe this is my life. All the hardships I have lived through have led me to find my forever. Finding the person you love feels like discovering a part of yourself you never knew was missing. It's like walking through life with a constant background hum, a subtle sense of incompleteness, and then suddenly, there they are. The hum quiets, replaced by a symphony of emotions you didn't know you were capable of feeling.

When I found Benson, it was like the world shifted slightly on its axis. Colors seemed more vibrant, sounds clearer, and every little detail of life felt significant. His presence brought a sense of calm I had never experienced before, as if his very being whispered to my soul, "You're home."

There were the small things, too—the way he looked at me with such genuine care, the warmth of his hand in mine, the way his laughter could light up a room and make my heart skip a beat. In his eyes, I saw a reflection of all the good things I hoped for in life, and I knew I had found someone special.

The idea of true love isn't born from fear but from an overwhelming sense of belonging. It's waking up each morning and knowing that, no matter what happens, there's a person who loves you unconditionally, flaws and all. It's the comfort of shared silences, the thrill of shared adventures, and the deep, unspoken understanding that you're in this together, no matter what.

With Benson, I feel a sense of security I've never known before. It's like he wraps me in an invisible embrace, shielding me from the harshness of the world. His love is my anchor, grounding me when things get tough, and his presence is a constant reminder that I am not alone.

There are days when I look at him and my heart feels so full it could burst. It's in those moments that I realize how deeply I've fallen for him and how fiercely I want to hold on to this feeling. It's not about clinging out of desperation but about cherishing something so precious that you can't imagine life without it.

To truly love someone is to choose them every day, through every joy and every challenge. It's knowing that, come what may, they are your person, your safe harbor, your greatest adventure. And it's a promise, spoken or unspoken, to be there, always, as they are for you.

"Ben! Dinner is ready," I called.

"My legs hurt even when I walk slowly. What are we having?" Ben asked.

"Some leftover pasta from yesterday," I
replied.

"Nice! That was the best dinner you've
cooked in weeks," he said.

"That's not true. What about the lasagna
recipe I followed the other day?" I responded.

"That too! I love everything you make,
especially when it's made with love," he said,
giving me a kiss.

"Well, today we are having some pre-heated
love," I said.

"Oh, I like the sound of that," he said.

"Ben! Not in front of our pasta," I said.

He laughed, and I instantly laughed back.

"Is this the life you imagined having?" Ben
asked.

"Waking up next to you is exactly how I
pictured my life. You are the person I dream
about. I have no doubts that you are perfect for
me," I confessed.

"Life is beautiful with you by my side. You are exactly how I pictured my future wife: beautiful inside and out. I can't imagine doing life with anyone else. There's no one I would rather be with for the rest of my life. You are my forever," he said.

"I love you," I said. His words felt like a band-aid on my heart. He healed parts of me that I never imagined could be put back together. He is the light in my dark days.

"I love you more," he said.

I took a bite of my pasta, processing his beautiful words.

"I'm excited to finally meet your parents for Christmas. I can't wait to see who you act more like," I said, grabbing some of the penne pasta with my fork.

"Probably neither of them," he said.

We talked for a full hour. Despite all the time I have spent with him, I still continue to learn new aspects of him. Each day with him reveals new layers of his personality, interests, and dreams. It's like peeling back the pages of a book, each chapter more intriguing than the last. The more time we spend together, the more I appreciate the depth and complexity of who he is, and it makes me eager to discover what the future holds for us.

After dinner we both tackled the dishes. Ben rinsed them off in the sink as I loaded them in the dishwasher. We made a great team. That's how we saw our relationship develop knowing that he's always going to have my back.

We sat on our balcony, the cool evening air wrapping around us as we settled into our outdoor loveseat. The stars twinkled above, painting the night sky with a serene beauty. I rested my head on Benson's shoulder, feeling the steady rise and fall of his breath. There was something magical about moments like this, where the world seemed to slow down just for us.

"Benson," I said softly, breaking the comfortable silence.

"Yeah?" he replied, his voice a gentle murmur as he turned slightly to look at me.

"Do you ever think about how we ended up together? Like, if our paths aligned for a reason?" I asked, gazing up at the stars.

He was quiet for a moment, as if considering the weight of my question. "I do, actually," he said finally. "I think about it a lot. There were so many little things that could have gone differently, but they didn't. We found each other despite everything."

I nodded, feeling a warm rush of emotion. "It's strange, isn't it? How one decision, one moment, can change everything. Sometimes I wonder if it's all part of some bigger plan."

Benson shifted slightly, his arm wrapping around me, pulling me closer. "Maybe it is," he said thoughtfully. "Or maybe it's just luck, or fate, or whatever you want to call it. But I do believe that we were meant to find each other. It just feels too perfect to be random."

I smiled, feeling his words resonate deep within me. "I like that idea," I said softly. "That we're part of something bigger. That all the struggles and challenges led us to this point."

He pressed a gentle kiss on my lips. "Me too, Madison. And no matter what brought us together, I'm just glad it happened. I can't imagine my life without you."

I felt a surge of love for him, this man who had become my everything. "I can't imagine mine without you either, Benson. You've brought so much joy and strength into my life. I feel like we make each other better."

"We do," he agreed. "We're stronger together. And I'm grateful every day that our paths crossed."

I used to think true love was something that happened to other people, something you read about in books or saw in movies. But then, Benson came into my life, and everything changed. It wasn't just the way he looked at me, but the way he saw me—truly saw me.

When I first met Benson, I was still grappling with my new reality as a paraplegic. I felt broken, incomplete, and lost in a world that suddenly seemed full of barriers. I had built walls around my heart, convinced that no one could ever see past my wheelchair to the person I really was. But Benson did.

From the moment our paths crossed, there was a spark between us, something that felt both familiar and excitingly new. He never saw my disability as a limitation. Instead, he saw my strength, my resilience, and my spirit. Where I saw obstacles, he saw opportunities. Where I felt insecure, he offered unwavering support and encouragement.

Benson had this incredible way of making me feel like I was the most important person in the world. He made me laugh, listened to my fears, and celebrated my victories, no matter how small. It was like he saw straight through to my soul, understanding parts of me I hadn't even fully understood myself.

True love, I've come to realize, always finds its way. It's not about perfection or fairy tales. It's about connection, understanding, and acceptance. It's about seeing someone for who they truly are, beyond the surface. Benson did that for me. He saw the woman behind the wheelchair, the dreams behind the doubts, and the heart behind the scars.

He taught me that love isn't about fixing what's broken; it's about embracing it, cherishing it, and finding beauty in the imperfections. With him, I learned to love myself again, to see my worth and my potential. Benson was my mirror, reflecting back all the good things I had forgotten about myself.

In his eyes, I found a home, a sanctuary where I could be my true self without fear or judgment. He made me believe in love again, the kind that endures, that grows stronger with every challenge. Our journey together has been a testament to the power of true love, to its ability to heal, to uplift, and to transform.

Love found us when we least expected it, weaving its way through the twists and turns of our lives, bringing us together in the most unexpected and beautiful way. And in Benson, I found not just a partner, but a kindred spirit, someone who saw me, accepted me, and loved me completely. True love found its way to us, and for that, I am eternally grateful.

Chapter 25
Day By Day

Three years later

Norway had always been a dream destination for me, a place of ethereal beauty and untamed landscapes. And now, here I was, exploring it with Benson by my side. We had spent the past few days traversing lush valleys, marveling at majestic fjords, and losing ourselves in the charm of quaint villages, all while ensuring the paths were accessible for my wheelchair.

Today, we decided to visit a lake renowned for its breathtaking scenery. The path was a well-maintained trail, smooth and wide enough for my wheelchair. The towering pine trees flanked the trail, their earthy scent mingling with the crisp, fresh air. Birds chirped overhead, and the distant sound of a waterfall added a serene soundtrack to our journey.

Benson held my hand, his warmth grounding me as he walked beside me, occasionally giving my wheelchair a gentle push when the terrain required it. Every now and then, he would stop to point out a unique flower or an interesting rock formation. His enthusiasm was infectious, and I found myself falling more in love with him and this beautiful country with each passing moment.

As we rounded a bend, the trees parted, revealing the lake in all its glory. My breath caught in my throat. The water was a perfect mirror, reflecting the snow-capped mountains that framed it. The sky above was a vibrant blue, with fluffy white clouds lazily drifting by. Wildflowers in a riot of colors dotted the shore, their reflection creating a kaleidoscope of hues on the water's surface.

"It's even more beautiful than I imagined," I whispered, squeezing Benson's hand.

He smiled, his eyes twinkling with the same awe that I felt. "It's perfect," he said softly.

We made our way to a large, flat viewing platform near the water's edge and settled there, our feet dangling just above the surface. The tranquility of the place seeped into my bones, and I felt an overwhelming sense of peace.

Benson reached into his backpack and pulled out a small thermos of hot chocolate. "I thought this might be nice with this weather," he said, pouring us each a cup. The rich, sweet aroma mingled with the fresh scent of the lake, creating a heady mix that was both comforting and invigorating.

I took a sip, the warmth spreading through me. "This is perfect," I said, leaning my head on his shoulder. "I don't think I've ever felt this content."

He wrapped his arm around me, his fingers gently stroking my arm. "I'm glad you're happy," he murmured. "There's nowhere else I'd rather be than here with you."

We sat in silence for a while, simply soaking in the beauty around us. The only sounds were the gentle lapping of the water against the shore and the occasional call of a distant bird. Time seemed to stand still, and I wished I could capture this moment and hold onto it forever.

Benson looked out at the shimmering water, a thoughtful expression on his face. "You know, moments like this make me realize just how beautiful life is."

I nodded, following his gaze. "I was thinking the same thing. It's incredible how nature has a way of grounding us, reminding us of what really matters."

He turned to me, his eyes soft and filled with warmth. "Being here with you, surrounded by all this beauty… it makes me appreciate every little thing. Life can be so chaotic, but these moments of peace are what make it all worth it."

I reached out and took his hand, intertwining our fingers. "I feel the same way. It's like all the worries and stresses fade away, and we're just here, together, in this perfect moment."

As the sun began to dip below the horizon, casting a golden glow over the lake, Benson turned to me, his expression serious. "Madison," he said, his voice filled with emotion. "Being here with you, seeing you so happy makes me realize how lucky I am. I'm in love with you.

Tears welled up in my eyes, and I reached out to touch his cheek. "I love you too, Benson. More than anything."

He leaned in, his lips meeting mine in a kiss that was as tender and profound as the landscape around us. In that moment, surrounded by the raw beauty of Norway, I knew that no matter where life took us, we would always have this perfect memory, a testament to our love and the magic of the world we shared.

Ben's phone started ringing.

"It's my mom," he said.

"Answer it. While you take the call I'm going to make a quick journal entry here in front of the lake," I said.

"I'll be right back so I won't disturb you," he said, getting up.

I took my lavender-colored journal and a pen from my bag and started to write:

*Dear Mom,*

*I made it to Norway. It's beautiful here! It was fun seeing all the places where Benson spent most of his years studying. Nature here looks untouched. You can hear birds chirping and the sounds of wild animals everywhere you go. The lakes and mountains look like computer wallpapers. I swear the shades of blues and greens here look different. People are also different here. They don't live in a fast-paced environment like we do back home. I wish you were here to experience this with me.*

I'm doing well, in case you were worried. You were right! Ben is an amazing guy. He loves me unconditionally, and we both take care of each other. We got married this past year. It was a beautiful, small wedding, just like I always wanted. We are planning to have a baby soon. Can you believe it? Soon I will become a mom, just like you. I'm scared and excited at the same time, but I know that Ben is going to be an amazing father. I see it every day.

Dad is doing well. He finally gave himself permission to explore love again, and he looks happy. I'm happy for him.

Thank you for all you did for me. You are always on my mind and in my heart. I kept your promise. I'm still going. Life is hard sometimes, but I keep taking it day by day like you taught me. I promise I'll make sure that your grandkids know how beautiful and special you were. I love you, Mom. I miss you. I have to go now. I'm going to love you and miss you forever.

Farewell,

Madison

# Connect with the Author

Steven Torres is a Puerto Rican author. He holds a Bachelor's Degree in Office System Management. "Farewell to Forever" marks his debut as a self-published novelist.

Email
steventorresborrero@gmail.com

Connect with him on social media

@steventorresbooks